WAR GIRL LOTTE

WAR GIRL SERIES, BOOK 2

MARION KUMMEROW

War Girl Lotte, War Girl Series, Book 2

Marion Kummerow

Cover Design by http://www.StunningBookCovers.com

READER GROUP

Marion's Reader Group

Sign up for my reader group to receive exclusive background information and be the first one to know when a new book is released.

http://kummerow.info/subscribe

CONTENTS

CHAPTER 1

Germany, September 1943

Lotte Klausen rushed down the stairs and into the kitchen only seconds after she woke up. Near the stove, Aunt Lydia and her five children stood in line, youngest to oldest like stair steps. Washed, combed, and adorable like never before.

The moment Lotte flew inside, they opened their mouths in unison and sang "Happy Birthday," their sweet little voices filling the room. Despite Lotte's disgruntlement about having to spend her birthday in some godforsaken village in Upper Bavaria, far away from her family in the capital, she was moved to tears.

"Happy seventeenth birthday," Aunt Lydia beamed and pressed Lotte against her belly, swollen with cousin number six. Her children did the same, and Lotte could barely breathe from being hugged by so many warm bodies at the same time.

"Open presents," Maria, the two-year-old, demanded.

"And blow out the candles on your cake," another cousin added.

On a signal from Aunt Lydia, her cousins obediently stepped aside, and Lotte stared with awe at the cream gateau, topped generously with whipped cream, fresh blackberries, and two lit candles in the shapes of a 1 and a 7. No doubt Lydia had made the candles herself.

"Thank you so much." Lotte blinked tears of emotion away, then blew out the candles, closed her eyes, and made her secret birthday wish.

I want to leave this godforsaken village.

"What you wish? What you wish?" Maria hopped up and down while pulling on Lotte's skirt.

Lotte put a finger to her lips, giving her a secret smile. "You know I can't tell, or it won't come true."

The children giggled as Lydia gestured toward the chair at the head of the table. "Aren't you going to sit down?"

"Of course, forgive me, Aunt. The cake looks wonderful." After taking her seat, she reached for her first present. It was from her mother, and as she opened it, she wished she could be with her family in Berlin. Before she could blink it away, a single tear rolled down her cheek as she remembered happier times before the war. Times when they'd all lived together – Mutter, Vater, her older siblings, Ursula, Anna, and Richard. Her father and her brother, who was one year older than Lotte, had both exchanged the family apartment for the trenches, and they hadn't heard from them in months.

She added a second birthday wish to the first. *Please, let Vater and Richard come home safely.*

Carefully opening the adhesive tape with a knife Aunt Lydia handed her, Lotte unwrapped the box and smoothed the wrapping paper before handing it to her aunt. Forever frugal, Lydia would save it to be reused.

A beautiful summer dress lay on the table. It was an off-white cotton adorned with bunches of bright-red cherries with green leaves. The fitted bodice and capped sleeves looked so mature, Lotte couldn't wait to try it on.

"It's a beautiful dress," Lydia said, stroking the fabric with her fingers while warning her children not to do the same.

"Yes, it is. And look, the pleated skirt will make it swing." *If only I had somewhere fun to wear it.* "Oh, it's going to look so pretty on me."

"Open your other presents," her aunt said.

Lotte nodded and reached for the package from her sisters, carefully unwrapping the paper.

"Oh my goodness, look at them!" she exclaimed and held up a pair of brand new plimsolls. They were light brown and sturdy with rubber soles.

Lydia couldn't have looked more pleased for her. "Your sisters chose a good gift."

Lotte looked down at her old shoes, the pink flesh of her toes peeking out where the sole and body of the shoes had separated. Her feet had grown this last year, as had the rest of her. She pushed her worn shoes off and slid the new ones on, wiggling her toes inside as she laughed in delight. "They're perfect!"

Aunt Lydia smiled and handed her one more package. "This one is from me."

Knowing the sacrifices her aunt had most likely made to gift this to her, she took the box reverently in her hands. "Thank you." Lotte opened the package and smiled at the bright yellow pinafore her aunt had sewn for her. "Oh! It's lovely."

Lydia beamed. "I'm glad you like it. You can wear it while doing your chores, so your new dress won't get dirty."

Her cousins, ranging in age from two to ten, had grown tired of waiting and bounced in their chairs. "Open ours, Lotte. Open our gifts."

Lotte grinned and accepted the hand-painted pictures they held out to her. She oohed and aahed over them until it was finally time for cake.

Maria climbed into her lap, her thumb tucked into her mouth. "I liked your painting, Maria," Lotte said, giving the little girl a tight squeeze.

Maria nodded, never removing the thumb from her mouth. Lotte laughed and then thanked each of the other children. "Your paintings are beautiful."

Lydia handed her the first slice of cake, and Lotte took a bite, closing her eyes as the sweet treat melted in her mouth. "It's delicious."

Soon, everyone had their own piece of cake and the only sound filling the kitchen was the chewing of seven mouths. The children were excused from the table as soon as they'd finished, but Lotte hung back with her aunt. "Thank you for the pinafore and the cake. I haven't eaten anything so delicious in ages."

Lydia sighed. "I was lucky. I managed to trade a chicken

for honey. Our sugar rations weren't nearly enough for the cake." Since the farmhand had joined the *Wehrmacht*, and her husband had been drafted shortly thereafter, she ran the farm on her own, with nothing more than the help of her ten-year-old son and two of his friends. On top of that, she raised five children, carried another one, and had taken in her niece.

At thirty years of age, Lydia had the calloused hands and the weathered face of an old woman. She wore her long, thick blonde hair braided into snails above her ears, making her look even more strict.

"This war can't go on forever," Lotte said, putting on her new pinafore. While she loved the bright color and the consideration Lydia had put into the gift, she hated the way it reminded her that she had to stay with her aunt instead of her parents. She swirled around and glanced at her aunt. "It's about time someone chased those Nazis away."

"Hush," her aunt scolded. "It's talk like that that got you sent up here in the first place."

Lotte made a face, but she held back what was in her mind. After a small pause, she asked, "Could I call my mother and sisters on the telephone, please?"

"You'll have to wait until this evening, but since it's your birthday, you may."

"Thank you."

Even though she'd managed to keep her response calm and even, anger flooded Lotte's body. Instead of living in the exciting capital of Berlin, doing all kinds of exciting things, her mother had banished her to the country. For two and a half years, she'd been stuck in the forlorn village of Kleindorf with a population of fewer than one hundred souls – including the dogs. And whose fault was that?

"If it wasn't for those damned Nazis, I wouldn't have to beg for permission to make a telephone call. I would be living happily in Berlin with my family." Lotte trembled with the outburst of emotion, and tears of anger wetted her eyes.

Lydia stopped clearing the table and glared at her. "Charlotte Alexandra Klausen. You keep quiet. One day, your sharp tongue and rash behavior are going to get you into real trouble, and I don't want to be the one who has to tell your mother when that happens."

Because she'd received similar warnings many times before, Lotte only shrugged her shoulders nearly to her ears. What could happen to her? Seriously? In this boring village, the biggest danger was to be accidentally kicked by a cow while milking her.

Later that evening, she called her mother's home and grinned when Anna answered. Anna was the middle sister, four years older than Lotte, with straight blonde hair that made her look demure, like an angel – when she was anything but.

Her sister was strong-willed, ambitious, and ferociously independent. At the age of ten, after two years of dissecting frogs, snails, and other insects, she'd announced that she was going to be a scientist, a human biologist. The choice had caused her parents much anxiety, since it was a totally inappropriate profession for a woman. After years of fighting against her parents' conservative mindset as well as the Nazi ideal of the demure and obedient *Hausfrau*, Anna had relented and trained as a nurse. Lotte suspected this was just a temporary defeat. No doubt, when the war was over, Anna would pursue her dream again.

"Happy birthday, little sister," Anna congratulated, her voice sounding tinny over the line.

"Thank you. And thank you so much for the plimsolls. They are amazing. They fit like a glove. Smashing."

A giggle pierced her ear. "Glad you like them. How's your life over there?"

"Don't even ask," Lotte pouted into the phone; then she lowered her voice. "I can't talk right now, but if nothing happens soon, I might die of boredom."

Anna laughed. "Come on, it can't be that bad. And you wouldn't want to be in Berlin right now with air raids every other night."

"You have no idea." Lotte sighed into the phone and glanced at her feet. At least now she had nicely fitting plimsolls without holes. A definite plus for the next race against her cousins.

"Do you want to talk to Ursula and Mutter?" Anna asked.

She wanted to talk for hours with her sister but knew her time was already growing short. "Yes, please."

"Happy birthday, Lotte." The oldest at twenty-two, Ursula was blessed with the same blonde hair as the rest of the family, apart from Lotte. Lotte was a fiery redhead with golden strands from the sun. At least Ursula shared her curls. But while Lotte's mane was untamable on the best days and an outright mess on bad days, Ursula somehow managed to comb her hair into elegant waves.

"Thank you. It's so good to hear your voice."

"How's my baby sister?" Ursula asked. Usually, Lotte

hated to be called *baby*, but today she missed her sisters so much, she didn't rise to the bait.

"Considering the circumstances, I'm fine," Lotte answered in a grave voice.

"The circumstances are utter boredom, I suppose?" Ursula chuckled into the phone and Lotte couldn't help but laugh with her. "Come on, sweetie, let me get Mutter for you."

Lotte waited, and a moment later her mother's voice came across the line. "Charlotte, darling! Happy birthday, my sweet girl."

The words were like a warm cloak wrapping itself around her shoulders. "Thank you, Mutter. The dress is so beautiful."

"I hope it fits you."

"It fits perfectly." Lotte was wearing the new dress and moved her hips to make the skirt swing, although her mother couldn't see it. "And I love the way it swings around my knees. It's smashing."

It was her new favorite word.

"Smashing?" Lotte *saw* the way her mother raised her eyebrow at her choice of words. "Are you behaving and not giving Lydia grief?"

"Of course, Mutter. But please, when can I return home?" Two and a half years in the countryside felt like a lifetime, and Lotte had more dreams for her life than milking cows or harvesting crops.

"Oh, sweetheart. We've been over this so many times. You're too outspoken and headstrong. One negative comment about the current regime heard by the wrong person, and you could endanger not only yourself but the entire family."

"I hate it here," Lotte whispered. Aunt Lydia was kind, and Lotte loved her cousins, but it wasn't the same as being with her own family.

"I wish you could be here, too, but for now Aunt Lydia's is the safest place for you."

"Fine. But only until the war is over, right?" Lotte wondered what would happen if Hitler won the war. Would she have to live in this forlorn place for the rest of her days? God, no! Something had to give.

"We'll see. Can you please let me talk to Lydia for a moment?"

"Of course." Feeling forlorn, Lotte called her aunt.

Lydia was her mother's youngest sister, and more than a decade ago, she'd married the son of a farmer and moved with him to Kleindorf.

Lotte handed her aunt the receiver and left the room. With watery eyes, she changed into the pinafore and went to the stable to milk the cows. The chores didn't care that it was her birthday.

CHAPTER 2

The summer was exceptionally hot, and Lotte and her two oldest cousins hurried to finish their chores. In the heat of the afternoon, they headed for a nearby pond surrounded by large trees. After frolicking in the cool water for a while, they stretched out on the grass to be dried by the sun.

Lotte glanced at her new plimsolls. A grin spread across her face, and she couldn't resist the challenge.

"First up the tree wins," she shouted at her cousins and tied the shoelaces as fast as she could. Clad in her bathing costume and wonderful birthday shoes, she ran for the highest tree and climbed from branch to branch, like Tarzan.

"I beat you," Lotte announced in a sing-song voice as soon as she reached the top with a hammering heart.

Jörg, her eldest cousin, shot her a dirty look. "That's because you got those smashing new plimsolls. Otherwise–"

"Excuses, nothing but excuses," Lotte teased and cheered for herself, "I always win. I'm the fastest and best climber around."

They climbed back to the ground and cooled their scratched hands and knees in the pond. Much too soon, the church bell chimed six times.

"We better go back, or we'll be in trouble with Mom," Jörg said. Despite his ten-and-a-half years, he shouldered most of the heavy labor on the farm and oftentimes acted as if he were the man of the house.

"Yes, ignoring our chores won't give us bonus points." Lotte slipped into her pinafore, and they raced each other back to the farm. She grabbed the milk pail and the wooden stool as she entered the large structure, the cows already forming a queue.

"What's your name again? Was it Maribelle or Bess?" she addressed the first cow in line, but the cow didn't seem to have an opinion one way or the other. Not even a moo indicated her preference. Lotte filled the pail and then poured the milk into the strainer near the barn door to cool and separate. The next day she'd ladle the cream, and Aunt Lydia would churn it into butter.

Since Uncle Peter and the farmhand had both been drafted years ago, no grown-up men resided on the farm, and all the children, except for the two youngest, had to chip in with the chores. Lotte's daily task was to take care of the animals – milking the cows, collecting the eggs from the hen house, feeding the hens and the sows. Sandra tended the vegetable and herbs garden while Jörg was in charge of the tractor, sowing, plowing, mowing, and whatever else needed to be done. Helmut cared for the vast orchard meadow.

At least one thing is better in Kleindorf than in the capital, Lotte thought as she licked the cream from her lips after taking a big sip of fresh, warm milk. In the few weeks she'd visited her family in January, she'd experienced firsthand how much better and more abundant the food was on Lydia's farm than what could be obtained with the ration cards in Berlin.

Returning to her milking duties, she moved the stool and began to milk the next cow. She was so absorbed in her work that she hadn't seen anyone approach and jumped, almost knocking over the pail, when she suddenly heard footsteps.

"Lotte?" a low voice asked.

Lotte looked around but couldn't see anyone, her heart hammering hard against her ribs. "Yes. Who are you? And where?"

"It's me, Rachel." A skinny girl Lotte's age with dark brown hair and brown eyes appeared.

"You gave me a fright." Lotte smiled at her neighbor, but her smile fell moments later when she noticed the terror in the girl's eyes and the dried tears on her cheeks. "Rachel, what's wrong? What's happened?"

Rachel sank down onto the straw floor and sobbed. "They arrested my parents today, and Herr Keller has taken over our farm." Herr Keller was not only the mayor of the district town, Mindelheim, but also the Chief of Police and Party leader.

"What? Why would they arrest your parents?" Lotte

blurted out. "They've done nothing wrong." Of course, she knew that anyone could be arrested for anything in the big cities. But here in Kleindorf? This had never happened before. People here minded their own business, worked on their farms, and stayed out of politics. Most of the time, anyway.

Rachel's parents were Aunt Lydia's closest neighbors, their farm only about half a mile down the road. But since Rachel and her three younger siblings had been expelled from school for being Jewish, Lydia had warned her own children and Lotte to keep their distance.

Rachel quietly sobbed on the ground, not offering any answer. And there really was no answer needed. Jews didn't have to do anything wrong. They *were* wrong, simply by birth.

"Someone needs to tell that awful man to mind his own business. What gives him the right to go around stealing peoples' homes?" Lotte railed against Herr Keller.

The sobbing intensified, and Lotte switched her focus to the more immediate concern. "Do you know where they took your parents?"

It took a few moments until Rachel was able to speak, but even then, her voice was strained with raw emotion. "I followed them at a safe distance and saw them pushed onto one of those big train wagons. You know the ones they use for cattle?"

Lotte nodded, not speaking aloud what they both knew. People who got on the cattle cars were never seen or heard from again. Nobody knew where they took them, but it certainly wasn't a nice place.

"Where are your brothers and sister? Did they take them

too?" Lotte hugged the desperate girl, who might have been her classmate – friend even – in other times.

Rachel shook her head. "We were just returning from collecting berries and mushrooms in the woods. I told them to run and hide. Since the last cow died, and we couldn't get any seeds to plant this year, we've only had the rations they give us."

"I'm so sorry." Lotte hugged her once more. She knew that Jews received reduced rations and were always served last.

"Lotte, we need a place to hide," Rachel said, wiping her face with the backs of her hands.

"I'll ask Aunt Lydia." Lotte didn't think twice before she offered. "Find your brothers and sister and meet me in the barn in an hour."

"Thank you." The relief in Rachel's big brown eyes was overwhelming.

Lotte dashed to the house as fast as her feet would carry her. "Aunt Lydia? Aunt Lydia? Where are you?"

"In the kitchen," her aunt shouted back. "What's all the fuss?"

Lotte stumbled inside, breathless from running too fast. "Rachel and her brothers and sister…they need a place to stay…can they live here, please?"

Lydia's lips thinned with every word Lotte spoke, her eyes growing wide in pure terror. "No. What are you thinking?"

It wasn't the answer Lotte expected, and she looked at her loving aunt like she was a stranger. "But her parents have been arrested, and this awful Herr Keller has taken over their farm. He thinks just because they're Jewish he can steal their home!" Lotte puffed out. When she'd finally told the entire story, her aunt shook her head with a stern expression on her face.

"We can't take them. They are fugitives from the law. They need to turn themselves in."

"But–"

Lydia put up a warning finger. "No buts. Even if I wanted to offer them shelter, I couldn't. I have to think about my children, about you. What would happen if someone found them?" She raised an eyebrow, searching for an answer.

Lotte's stomach churned. "I don't know–"

"Well, let me tell you. I would be arrested for obstructing justice. Some Party member would come and take over my farm while you, Helmut, and Jörg would serve the new owners as farmhands and the three little ones would be sent to an orphanage. There's more at stake than just Rachel and her siblings. As much as I regret this, blood is thicker than water, and I have to do what's best for my family."

Lotte returned with a hanging head to the barn to give Rachel the bad news. But when she looked into four pairs of hopeful eyes, she couldn't.

"You can stay in the barn. But nobody can know you're here, not even my aunt."

Rachel's face was strained with uncertainty. "But Lotte–"

"No buts. You'll stay here until we find another place for you. For the time being, you're safe here. Nobody comes in here but me."

Rachel's fingers twisted, her anxiety clear in her every movement. "Are you sure? Maybe we should turn ourselves in? It might not be so bad where they're taking us."

Goosebumps rose on Lotte's arms as she remembered the stories she had heard. She gave her friend a very serious look. "I wouldn't want to find out."

CHAPTER 3

The next morning, Lotte got up before everyone else and slipped into the pantry, where she took a few crusts of bread, some cheese, and a chunk of sausage. Hiding everything in her pinafore, she passed by the vegetable garden, picking a few things here and there, adding them to the other provisions. Then she slipped into the barn.

Nobody showed up. *They're probably still asleep, poor little things.* As much as she wanted to wait and talk to Rachel and the other three children, she had to continue her normal routine. Any change would only alert Aunt Lydia that something was amiss.

She fetched her milking stool and left the offerings where she was sure Rachel would see them, including a note that she would see her at nightfall. As soon as she finished her morning chores, Lotte changed into her new dress and asked her aunt if she could visit a friend in Mindelheim. Since it was a Saturday and the corn and silage harvest hadn't begun yet, her aunt agreed, under the condition that Lotte would be back in time for the evening chores.

Lotte hopped on her bicycle and fiercely pedaled the six miles into town. On the last mile, the road rose steeply, and by the time she reached the market square, her cheeks were burning with heat and sweat had dampened her dress. Breathing heavily, she came to a stop in front of Irmhild's house.

Irmhild must have seen her coming because she dashed out of the front door even before Lotte had parked her bicycle. Her long light-brown braids framedd her face on either side "Lotte. I had hoped you'd come by. Happy belated birthday." She gave her friend a hug and grimaced. "Ugh, you're all sweaty. I don't understand why you can't push your bicycle up the hill like everyone else."

"Because it's faster and more fun to pedal." Lotte wiped her forehead with the back of her hand.

The look on Irmhild's face was evidence of her opinion about the *fun* part. "Speaking of fun, want to get some ice cream and go down by the river? My treat for your birthday."

"Ice cream?" Lotte giggled and linked arms with her friend. "Who would say no to such an offer? Certainly not me."

Irmhild had been in Lotte's class until she left school earlier this year to start working at the town hall. Since Mindelheim was the district town, it handled everything from birth certificates and identification papers to ration cards, weddings, taxes, and state pensions. Even property titles and death certificates passed through its doors.

Five minutes later, the friends arrived at the market

square. Despite being the district town, Mindelheim was a tiny place with only five thousand inhabitants. Irmhild bought two cones of ice cream for them, and they ate the rare treat while crossing the cobblestone square with the big fountain in the center. Passing the town hall, the grocery shop, the hardware store, and the church, they reached the dirt path down to the river. When they arrived, they both shucked their shoes and socks and sat on the riverbank, dangling their feet in the cool water.

"Do you know when school starts this autumn?" Lotte asked.

"No." Irmhild shook her head, making her braids swing like bell ropes. "Herr Keller, the mayor, said maybe it never will. Most of the boys have been drafted during the summer break, and there's no need for higher education for the girls."

Lotte sighed. This meant more boredom for her. But most of her classmates had dropped out of school anyway. They were needed at home or as workers on the farms.

"So, what are you going to do after the summer?" Irmhild asked.

"If it were up to me to decide, I'd leave this place."

"But to do what?" Irmhild leaned back on her elbows, raising her face to the sun.

"Who cares? Anything is better than being stuck on a farm in the middle of nowhere." Lotte took a pebble and sent it skipping across the water.

"It's not that bad; at least we have enough food and a warm bed."

Lotte turned and looked into Irmhild's blue eyes. She was her only friend, apart from her cousins. Most people didn't understand why the two of them had become friends. On the outside, they were opposites. While Lotte was impulsive, outspoken, and always up for a fight, Irmhild was quiet, thoughtful, and tried to accommodate everyone. But despite those differences, they shared the ambition to become more than a wife and mother.

Although she was in the *Bund Deutscher Mädel*, the Hitler Youth organization for girls, Irmhild didn't agree with most of the Nazi ideology. She just didn't voice her concerns aloud.

Lotte took another pebble and tossed it into the water. After watching the ripples until they reached the shore, she murmured, "You remember Rachel?"

"Yes, why?" Irmhild's voice was languid, but even without looking at her, Lotte sensed the tension building between them.

"Her parents were arrested yesterday and sent off in one of the cattle trains."

A sharp intake of air was the only answer from her friend.

Lotte stared at the lazily flowing river. "Rachel came last night while I was milking the cows. She was with Aron, Israel, and Mindel in the woods when it happened. They can't go back. Herr Keller has taken over their farm."

"He's been after that piece of land for years," Irmhild said. The tension between them was suffocating now, and neither one dared to look the other one in the eyes.

"It's so unjust!" Lotte jumped up and stomped her foot. "Why is he even allowed to do this? Go around stealing other people's homes? I hate–"

"Shush, Lotte." Irmhild grabbed her hand. "Sit down again, or you'll draw attention to us."

Lotte shot her a dirty look but obeyed. After a long silence, Irmhild raised her voice again, "Where are they now?"

Lotte looked around to see if they had gained unwelcomed eyes and ears. "Can you keep a secret?" When Irmhild nodded, she whispered, "They're hiding in the barn."

"What? In your aunt's barn?"

Lotte nodded, chewing her bottom lip.

"Does your aunt know?"

"No. Lydia said we can't shelter them, it would be too dangerous."

"Well, I hate to say it, but your aunt is right. Do you have any idea what would happen if anyone finds them? Herr Keller would happily take over your aunt's farm as well."

Lotte ran her hand through her wild curls. Irmhild always imagined the worst possible outcome. Nobody would find them, nothing would happen.

"They'll have to hide someplace else," Irmhild hissed.

"But where?" Lotte shivered at the helplessness in her own voice.

"They could stay with relatives."

Lotte snorted. "I don't think they have any left."

"An orphanage maybe?"

"What kind of orphanage takes Jewish children?"

"Hmm...but they can't stay in your aunt's barn. What should they eat? Without ration cards, they can't get anything."

"I snuck them some milk, cheese, bread, and a bit of sausage this morning."

"Ahh...and you think this is enough for four children? No, they can't stay hiding in the barn." A long silence ensued before Irmhild spoke again. "We have to find them a safe place to stay."

"But where?" Lotte buried her head in her hands. Yesterday, everything had seemed so easy. Rachel, Aron, Israel, and Mindel would hide in the barn until they could return to their farm. But after listening to Irmhild's words, she knew that was nothing less than impossible. Either they would starve to death, Aunt Lydia would question the missing provisions, or...

Icy chills ran down her spine as she remembered that harvest was about to start anytime soon. With dozens of people milling about the fields and barn, it was only a matter of time until someone found the children in hiding.

Loud voices from the other side of the river drew Lotte's attention, and she saw a group of elementary school children racing each other to the water.

"If they were Aryan, they would be safe," she murmured more to herself, but Irmhild's head flew around, and she stared at Lotte with wide-open eyes.

"You mean like getting them fake papers?" Irmhild asked.

Lotte hadn't considered that idea. "Now that you mention it, I think it's a great idea, but where would we get them?"

"At the town hall, of course," Irmhild blurted out, a terrified glance in her eyes following the initial enthusiasm.

"Yes, that's brilliant...but who?" Lotte cocked her head

and noticed the agitation in her friend. "Oh! You! Of course, you can do this. You work in the town hall. You do those things all the time. I mean, issuing papers and certificates."

"Actually not. I prepare everything, but Herr Keller has to sign the papers and put his official stamp on them." Irmhild rubbed her forehead. "I don't have access to the special paper we use for identification cards either."

"Can't you just sneak into his office, take four leaves of that paper, put the stamps on it and fake his signature? It can't be that hard, can it?" Lotte leaned forward, excitement buzzing through her veins. Finally, something might happen in this sleepy town. A real adventure.

Irmhild destroyed her hopes with a wild shaking of her head. "It's too dangerous, we should think of something else."

But after tossing ideas at each other for several more minutes, Lotte said, "There's no way around it. You have to make new Aryan papers for them. It's their only chance."

"But if Herr Keller ever notices..." Goosebumps sprang up on Irmhild's arms, and she didn't finish her sentence.

"He won't. Not if you're careful. And it's for a good cause. Don't you want Rachel and the others to be safe?"

Endless minutes passed by as Irmhild thought it all over. Just when Lotte feared she would go crazy with anticipation, her friend sighed. "All right. I'll do it, but you can't ever tell anyone. And you have to give them the papers. I can't be seen anywhere near Kleindorf."

"Now we're real spies. Isn't that exciting?" Lotte asked, giddy with enthusiasm.

"What is exciting?" a deep voice asked.

CHAPTER 4

Lotte's breath stuck in her lungs while her head flew around to face the direction of the voice. Two tall and strong boys her age stood a few feet apart, eyeballing the two girls. Both blond, they wore the uniform of the *Hitlerjugend,* a tan shirt with pockets, black shorts, and a black rolled neckerchief. The official insignia of Hitler's Youth movement – a swastika logo on an armband with red stripes bracketing a white stripe – adorned their right upper arms.

"None of your business," Lotte snapped at the older one.

But Hans Keller, the oldest son of the mayor, wasn't one to give up easily and cast her a lazy smile. "Come on, *Schätzchen,* we're neighbors now. Let me in on the fun."

"I'm not your darling." Lotte turned her head away. Hans had a way of making her neck hair stand on end with his behavior. He was so full of himself.

"But you could be, and it wouldn't be to your disadvantage." He moved close enough that the tips of his shoes were touching her thigh. Before Lotte could jump up and give him a piece of her mind, Irmhild put a calming hand on her arm.

"We were talking about Lotte's new dress," Irmhild said.

"You do look very nice today," the other boy complimented her. Uwe was the son of the forest warden and had dropped out of school earlier in the year to take over his father's duties while his father served at the front.

Lotte looked up. "Thanks, Uwe." During the last six months, Uwe had grown from a boy into a man. While he was a few inches shorter than Hans, his shoulders had broadened, and the muscles on his upper arms stretched the uniform shirt. No doubt, those muscles were a tribute to the hard work of felling trees and chopping wood.

For some reason, looking at Uwe made her feel lightheaded, and she quickly glanced to the side, where Hans stood and leered at her. She noticed the metal pin on Hans' shirt pocket.

So, he moved up in the ranks. I'll bet being the son of the chief of police and mayor helped in becoming the leader of the local Hitlerjugend.

"What if we give Lotte and her new dress an opportunity to be admired?" Hans asked, a cocky eyebrow raised. "There's a dance tonight in Kaufbeuren, and we could all go there."

"No. I can't." Lotte fisted her hand in her skirt. As much as she would love to attend a dance event, the idea of going with Hans caused the bile to rise in her throat.

Irmhild came to her aid. "I'm sorry, but my mother would never allow it either."

Hans gave an exaggerated sigh and flopped on the

ground beside Lotte. "So, we could go down to the pond for a swim?"

"Do you not understand the word *no*? Irmhild and I want to be left alone," Lotte said, sitting as upright as she could.

Uwe gave a dry chuckle, and Hans' smile fell. "There's no need to be rude."

"I wasn't trying to be rude, but we were having a conversation, and you interrupted it." Lotte swallowed. Inside she wasn't half as confident as her words conveyed.

"It's your loss, *Schätzchen*. One day you'll accept that you and I are destined for each other." Hans adopted a charming smile and blew her a kiss.

Lotte instinctively hunched her shoulders. "Watch me and wait!"

Hans watched her for another moment and then jumped to his feet again. "If that's what you want. Next time, then. Let's go, Uwe."

"See you around," Uwe said, and the two of them sauntered off.

"You shouldn't be so rude to Hans. It's not wise to have him and his father as enemies," Irmhild said once the boys were out of earshot.

"He gives me the creeps." Lotte threw back her red mane.

"I want to attract men like you do," Irmhild said, curling her mousy braid around her finger.

"Me? Except for Hans, no boy has ever showed any interest in me. And I can well do without him."

"Come on." Irmhild rolled her eyes. "Don't tell me you didn't notice that Uwe fancies you."

"I didn't." The heat rising to her cheeks and the strange

fluttering in her stomach told Lotte a different story. She and Uwe had been classmates before he dropped out of school, but today he had looked like an adult, nothing like the boy she knew.

"I tell you, it's true. And judging by the way you're blushing, you like him, too." Irmhild broke out into giggles, teasing her friend.

"All right. Uwe's cute, but he's friends with Hans, and he's part of the *Hitlerjugend*."

"They don't really have much of a choice. Every boy has to join up. Look at me, I'm part of the *Bund Deutscher Mädel*, and yet we two are still..." Irmhild lowered her voice to a conspiratorial whisper, "doing *these* things."

Lotte nodded and then looked up at the sky, where the sun was heading for the horizon. "I need to get back home."

Together, they walked to Irmhild's house, where Lotte had parked her bicycle. On an impulse, she hugged her friend tight. "Promise to be careful and give me a phone call when the papers are ready."

Irmhild's fingers twisted together. "Maybe it wasn't such a good idea," she answered with an unsteady voice.

"You can't back out now, you're Rachel's only hope. Nothing will happen." Lotte frowned at her friend.

"Let's hope so, my goodness." Irmhild opened the door and disappeared, leaving Lotte with a bad feeling. She shoved it aside, grabbed her bicycle and mounted it.

The way home was mostly downhill, and Lotte ducked low over the handlebars to gain speed until the wind ruffled her mane. For all she complained about being stuck in Kleindorf, she loved to roam about the landscape in a way that wasn't possible in Berlin.

Fifteen minutes later, she reached her aunt's farm and hurried to tackle her chores. The cows were already waiting patiently on the square in front of the barn to be milked. Lotte set aside some of the milk, several eggs, and vegetables before she slipped inside the barn to search for the four children.

She found them in the loft of the barn. Rachel still had puffy eyes, and the other children's faces were smeared with dirty tears.

"I brought you food." Lotte stared at the meager provisions in her hands. It was barely enough for one person, let alone four. Irmhild had been right; they couldn't stay in here for long. "I'm afraid you'll have to eat the eggs raw."

"Thank you. We won't stay here much longer. I just need to figure out where to go." Rachel took the food and carefully set it down on a straw bale.

Lotte seized Rachel's arm and pulled her out of earshot of the other children. "You remember Irmhild? She's working at the town hall and is making new papers for all of you."

Rachel's eyes all but popped out of her face. "Goodness. No. She can't do that! It is a crime, and if anyone finds out–"

"We thought about it, and it's the only way to keep you safe," Lotte insisted.

"Lotte! No. You have to stop her. What you're planning is much too dangerous," Rachel whispered with horror in her voice.

"Don't worry, Irmhild will be very careful. We won't get caught." Lotte grinned. It felt good to be a heroine.

Rachel shook her head. "I can't accept both of you

risking your lives for us. No, please call her tonight and tell her to stop. The risk is too great."

"Pah, what can happen to us? It'll work just fine, you wait and see."

But as Lotte walked to the main house, a bad feeling settled in her stomach. Her mother and her sisters had warned her once and again that every tiny act of opposition to the Nazi Party could get her imprisoned – or worse.

She shrugged and skipped to her room.

Adults are always afraid of one thing or the other.

CHAPTER 5

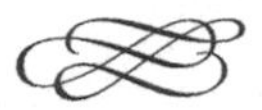

Two days had gone by, and Irmhild still hadn't called. Lotte wondered if her friend had forgotten about their plan – because it couldn't take that long to make some fake papers, right?

At the same time, she worried about Rachel and the other three children. They stayed hidden in the barn during the night but left before dawn to venture into the forest looking for something to eat. Mushrooms blackberries, wild garlic, hazelnuts, whatever edible things they could find to supplement the few provisions Lotte could sneak them.

By the afternoon, Lotte was dying from the uncertainty of not knowing what was happening. She picked up the telephone in the living room and called Irmhild.

"Town hall," her friend's voice came across the line.

"Irmhild, it's me."

"Lotte, you shouldn't be calling me at work." Her voice turned into a hiss.

Lotte shuffled her feet. "I know, and I'm sorry, but I was getting worried."

"Hold on a second," Irmhild said, her muffled voice indicating she was talking to someone else. After several minutes, she heard the sound of a door closing, and Irmhild's voice came back on the line. "It's more complicated than we thought. What we need is locked up, and I have to wait until someone comes in needing those same papers and the seal."

"I take it by your voice that hasn't happened yet?" Lotte asked.

"No. I wish I could tell you different. I'll let you know as soon as I can. I have to go now."

Irmhild hung up the phone and Lotte did the same, closing her eyes in dismay. This undertaking had turned out to be a lot more worrisome than she'd imagined.

She walked into the kitchen and poured herself a glass of water from the tap.

Aunt Lydia waddled into the house, puffing air. "I wish this baby would come already, I'm moving like a beached whale."

Lotte bit her lip to suppress a giggle and then eyed her aunt's belly suspiciously. It had grown so much during the last weeks, she feared it might explode any moment.

"Do you want some water, Aunt Lydia?"

"Yes. Thank you." Lydia sank down on a chair and gulped down the water Lotte handed her.

"Good to see you, Lotte. You'll have to clean out the barn in the next few days. I went into town and organized harvesters for next week."

"Next week?" Lotte almost dropped the glass. "Isn't that a bit early?"

"No. The weather has been exceptionally hot, and I want to have it done before this baby arrives." Lydia said and patted her belly.

"Oh," was all Lotte managed to say.

"I need you to sweep out the floors, clean the cobwebs and get everything ready to store the crops."

"I'll get on to it right away." Lotte dashed off to take stock of the situation in the barn. The refugees couldn't stay there, not when the harvest began. Work would sometimes continue until late at night, and people would notice if someone had slept in the fresh hay.

After dinner, she returned to bring Rachel the bad news. She found her in the loft, holding her sister on her lap and softly singing a lullaby to comfort the four-year-old. Lotte's heart squeezed at the sight. That poor child. She had no idea what was happening in the world and cried for her vanished mummy.

Rachel looked up at the shuffling of Lotte's feet and waved her forward. "Come and sit with me."

She looked so fragile and yet so much in control. Lotte wondered how she managed to take care of her baby sister and her two mischievous brothers the entire day, keeping them quiet and out of sight of everyone. She settled next to her and then quietly recounted the conversations with Irmhild and Lydia.

"If Irmhild doesn't get the papers before next week, I don't know how we're going to keep you hidden."

Rachel gave her a sad smile and shook her head. "Do not fret. We will leave and find someplace else."

"No!" Lotte shook her head. "I don't want you to leave until it is safe for you to do so. You need Aryan papers to guarantee safe passage."

"You've been so generous..." Rachel's eyes filled with tears.

"Don't cry, please," Lotte begged her. "I know Irmhild will come through. Everything will be fine."

"Maybe," Rachel murmured.

Lotte squeezed her hand and then climbed back down the ladder to the ground floor. After putting the milking equipment back where it belonged, she closed the sliding doors to the barn, her mind focused on the problem of Rachel.

"Ahhh," she shrieked when a young man appeared out of the shadows, blocking the pathway to the main house. She pressed her hand to her stomach when she recognized who it was. "What are you doing here, Hans?"

"Checking on you." He smirked.

"You're spying on me!" Lotte racked her brain, wondering if he might have been able to overhear her talking with Rachel.

"Are you doing something I should be spying on?" he asked with a teasing grin.

"I was doing my evening chores. What are you doing at my aunt's house?"

"I was in the area and wanted to see you. You weren't very nice to me the last time we saw each other. I thought without Uwe and Irmhild around you might be more accommodating."

Lotte shook her head and pushed past him, but Hans put out an arm, blocking her way and trapping her against the wall with his body. She froze, not sure whether this was one of his stupid pranks, but then he lifted a hand to her head and wrapped one of her strawberry blonde curls around his fingers.

She turned her eyes on him, glaring daggers of fury in his direction. "Take your hands off of me!"

"I like seeing you all riled up. Come for a walk with me," Hans chuckled.

"No."

"Lotte, come on. Be nice to me, and I'll be nice to you." His breath blew across the bare skin on her neck, and despite its warmth, she shuddered.

"I need to go inside," she insisted, trying to wriggle out of his embrace.

"Your aunt won't mind if she knows you're with me. What else do you have to do? I could help you finish your chores."

"I'm done with my chores, leave me alone!" Lotte did her best not to panic. If she screamed, nobody would hear her, except for Rachel.

"And if I don't want to?" Hans edged closer to her, his body heat and his masculine odor sending ripples of fear through her body. The next moment, he dipped his head and tried to kiss her, but she turned her face away, making his lips land on her cheek.

That's enough!

"Leave me alone." Lotte was shaking with fear and fury, but somehow, she managed to raise both hands and shoved at his chest as hard as she could.

He chuckled but retreated one step. "Come on, Lotte. I know you like me."

"Like you? I detest you. You're nothing more than a coward, flaunting your stupid Nazi uniform and hiding behind your father's coattails."

"You don't mean that!" Hans's voice had changed from teasing to menacing in an instant.

Lotte didn't respond but used his moment of shock to duck beneath his arm and dash for the safety of the farmhouse.

She ran as if the devil was at her back.

CHAPTER 6

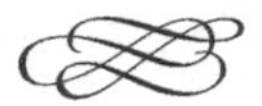

Three days later, Lotte parked her bicycle at the back of the town hall, which was already closed to the public, and rapped her knuckles on the door three times. Irmhild had called in the morning to tell her that she'd finally been able to steal the proper forms and had already sealed them.

The door opened a crack, and Lotte slid inside, her heart hammering with excitement. She'd barely been able to wait for this moment. Inside, it was eerily quiet, as the few employees had left for the day. Irmhild motioned to follow her to the basement.

"Why are we going downstairs?" Lotte asked, her footsteps clicking on the stone floor.

"Because I don't want anyone to see us through the windows," Irmhild answered and led her into a large room with overhead lighting.

"Oh! Good plan. So, you were able to get the papers sealed?"

"Yes. I used pictures of my brothers and me when we were children, but now I don't know what names to put on the papers. We can't use their real names, right?" Irmhild giggled nervously.

Lotte hadn't thought about that. But now it was obvious. Rachel Epstein wouldn't work well for an Aryan girl, and neither would the first names Israel, Aron, and Mindel. It dawned on her that there was a lot of detail she hadn't considered before embarking on this rash plan.

Down in the basement, Irmhild proudly showed her the identification papers she'd prepared. Giggling, they tossed around a few names until they settled for the first names of former classmates: Karin, Ingrid, Peter, and Klaus.

"Now, we just need to find a proper last name for them." Lotte sighed and tugged a wild strand behind her ear.

"That's easy. We'll use Müller. Half of the population is called Müller, so nobody will suspect anything." Irmhild carefully filled in the forms with the names, birth dates, and birthplaces. Then she blew on the ink and waved the paper in the air.

"Done. Give them to me. I'll take them to Rachel," Lotte offered.

"No, wait." Irmhild held the papers out of Lotte's reach. "The most important thing is still missing."

"What?" The new identifications looked surprisingly like the one Lotte carried in her bag.

"The mayor's signature. We have to forge it."

Lotte's jaw dropped. "You can do that, right?"

"No, but maybe if we practice, one of us can fake it." Irmhild produced a paper with Herr Keller's signature.

Lotte took a pen and blank paper and looked at the

mayor's signature for a moment. Herr Keller was not only the mayor, but also the Chief of Police, Party leader, and Hans' father. *Ugghh.* A queasy feeling settled in her stomach as she remembered her encounter with Hans the other night.

Her first attempt at forging the signature was a dismal failure, as was Irmhild's.

"This is not going well." Lotte looked at the signature again and tried for a heavier hand. After a dozen or more tries, she finally got the hang of it, and she held up the real signature and her fake one for Irmhild's inspection, "What do you think?"

"That's it! You did it!" Irmhild clapped her hands with excitement.

"Fine. Let's get these identifications signed. I need to get back to the farm before my aunt starts looking for me." When she was done, she admired her forgery work and grinned. "We're pretty good at this secret stuff."

Even Irmhild seemed to have stopped worrying for a moment. She smiled. "You're right. That's some fine work we've done here. And for a good cause."

"If my sisters could see this, I'll bet they would finally take me seriously." Lotte already dreamed of fame and fortune, but Irmhild grabbed her shoulder.

"Lotte, you can't tell anyone about this. No one. Ever!"

Lotte waved her concern off. "I know, I know...but imagine after the war is over. We'll be celebrated as heroines, everyone will admire us. We'll get invited to all the best parties." Her imagination was working overtime, and she got up, tossed back her wild curls and adopted a pinup girl pose. "Can't you just see the posters? Lotte Klausen and Irmhild Steinmetz. Female heroes of the war."

Irmhild giggled at her silliness and joined in, adopting a similar pose and blowing a kiss to her adoring fans. "I'll bet all of the boys coming back from the war would want to date us."

"We could go to exciting places, and everyone would want our autographs. Just like film stars." Lotte spun around in a circle, giggling in delight. Then she grabbed Irmhild's hands, and the two of them danced around the room. "This was fun."

Irmhild nodded, and after several more minutes of pure silliness, the two girls picked up their mess and prepared to exit the building. Irmhild hugged Lotte as they slipped out the back door of the town hall. "Ride home safely."

"I will. Talk to you soon." Lotte mounted her bicycle and pedaled fast all the way back to her aunt's farm. She managed to get her bike stowed in the barn and then settled in to milk the cows as if nothing had happened.

She itched to tell Rachel the good news, but nobody answered her quiet calls. Lotte tucked the fake papers inside a cubbyhole to keep them safe. Then she sauntered to the main house, smiling from ear to ear with the thrilling images of herself and Irmhild being celebrated as war heroes still fresh in her mind.

CHAPTER 7

"Aunt Lydia, I'm going to work in the barn for a while," Lotte called to her aunt right after breakfast. It wasn't normal for her to spend so much time in the barn, but with the harvest only days away, she knew no one would question her.

"Fine. I'm heading into town and taking your cousins with me. We'll be back this afternoon."

"See you later." Lotte took off for the barn, hoping the Epstein children hadn't left yet. She opened the door, pulled it shut behind her, and then smiled when she heard the sounds of Rachel's quiet voice coming from the loft.

Lotte retrieved the papers from their hiding spot and climbed the ladder. "Guess what I have?" She waved the papers in front of the children.

Rachel looked at her hand. "Papers?"

"Yes. Four brand new identification papers for the Müller children." Lotte handed over the precious things, beaming with pride.

"Thank you so much. Lotte, you don't know how much this means to us." Rachel's eyes filled with tears, but she rubbed them away and then hugged Lotte. One after another Israel, Aron, and Mindel came forward and did the same. Mindel was only four and didn't understand, but the faces of the seven- and ten-year-old boys showed that they knew way too much about the cruelties going on in this world.

"You're safe now." Lotte beamed at them and prepared to leave, but the scared look in Rachel's eyes held her back. "What's wrong?"

"Nothing. It's just…where should we go now? We can't return to my parents' farm with the Keller family living there. And…around here, everyone knows us. Even with these fake papers, we won't be safe."

"I hadn't thought about that." Lotte ran a hand through her long hair. *Again*. Her disappointment with herself grew. Maybe Mutter and Aunt Lydia were right, and she needed to think first instead of acting rashly. "I'll ask Irmhild. We'll think of something. Don't worry, everything will work out just fine."

But Lotte was much less confident than she pretended. What if things didn't work out? Would the possession of fake papers make everything worse for the Epstein children? Had she done them a disservice?

As much as she ached to rush into Mindelheim to talk with Irmhild, she couldn't leave the farm alone while Aunt Lydia was gone. And she couldn't call Irmhild at work either. No, this would have to wait until tomorrow morning.

When Aunt Lydia finally returned from town, it was

already time for dinner. This late in the summer, the sun settled too early to pedal into town and back with daylight. Since Lotte knew that her aunt didn't approve of Lotte riding her bicycle after nightfall, she decided not to ask and to visit Irmhild first thing in the morning.

Everyone settled around the kitchen table to eat cooked potatoes with butter and generous portions of home-baked bread. Aunt Lydia poured a glass of milk for each one of them before sitting down, a frown causing deep wrinkles in her forehead.

"The cows haven't been producing as much milk lately. Lotte, did you notice anything out of order?"

Lotte almost dropped the potato she'd just spiked with her fork. "Excuse me, Aunt Lydia?"

The frown grew even deeper. "When I went into town this morning, the leader of the farmer's association insinuated I was selling produce on the black market because I sold them considerably less milk and eggs last week than usual."

Lotte swallowed hard. All farmers were obligatory members of the *Reichsnährstand,* the ministry of agriculture. In towns like Mindelheim, the leader of the *Kreisbauernschaft,* the regional organization of the *Reichsnährstand,* was almost as powerful as the Party leader. "Now that you mention it, it has been so hot, and the grass on the meadows is getting brown and sparse. I'm sure once the temperature cools down they will be back to normal."

"One more reason to start the green fodder harvest. It has been unseasonably warm this year." Aunt Lydia wiped Maria's mouth and focused on her food.

Lotte cast her eyes downward, intent on not attracting

any undue attention to herself, and the issue of the cows and hens. She was relieved when Jörg started a conversation about the need to get diesel fuel for the tractor.

Soon, dinner was over, and Lotte sighed with relief when her aunt gave the order to clear the dinner dishes. Except for two-year-old Maria, all the other children had their tasks, and within minutes, dinner was cleaned up, and the kitchen was set to rights.

Aunt Lydia had just settled into the armchair, propping up her swollen feet on a stool and massaging her belly, when someone knocked on the door.

"Who could that be?" Lydia wondered and attempted to get up from the armchair.

"I'll get it. You sit and rest," Lotte called out and rushed to open the door. The next moment, she wanted to slam it into the faces of the unwelcome visitors.

"Good evening. It's Lotte, right?" Herr Keller asked, flanked by his wife and Hans.

"Yes." Lotte felt hot and cold shivers running up and down her spine.

"Who is it?" Lydia called from the living room.

"The mayor and his family," Lotte called back.

"Can we come in for a moment?" Herr Keller asked.

Finally, Lotte's brain had recovered from the shock and was able to think again. "Of course, Herr Keller, my aunt is resting."

She led the visitors into the living room, where her aunt rose from the armchair to greet them with much difficulty.

"Good evening, Herr and Frau Keller, what brings you here at this hour?" Lydia beamed at them, and Lotte couldn't tell if the expression was genuine or fake.

"A social call, Frau Schubert. We are your new neighbors and thought we would stop in to say hello." Herr Keller removed his hat and looked around the room.

"Please forgive me for not having visited with you earlier, but with preparing for the harvest next week and this baby due in less than a month..." Lydia pointed to her belly, "I've been too tied up here."

"No need to worry." Herr Keller smiled and took long, determined steps from one end of the living room to the other.

As if he's measuring the length, Lotte thought.

"We do understand the important role our farmers have in nourishing our people. People like you are the pillars of the Reich. In fact, my family and I have big plans for the farm we now own. Those dirty Jews left the land impoverished. It's a good thing they decided to leave."

Decided to leave? Lotte wanted to vomit on the mayor's shiny shoes.

Aunt Lydia must have sensed Lotte's inner turmoil because she sent her a warning stare and said, "Lotte, dear, can you please get our visitors some refreshments?"

"Of course, Aunt Lydia." Lotte bit her lip at all the other things she wanted to say. Her aunt was not a person to be trifled with.

Herr Keller sat down on the sofa, legs spread apart as if he owned the place, while his wife crouched beside him. Lotte overheard him and Lydia exchanging courtesies. Frau Keller was the proverbial Nazi wife, quiet and speaking only when spoken to.

When Lotte entered the living room again, a tray with three glasses of cold lemon balm tea in her hands, Herr

Keller had changed the topic to Hitler's recent successes and the imminent victorious end to the war.

"The capitulation of Italy was a shock, but considering how unreliable as allies they were in the first place, it's actually a blessing in disguise. The glorious Wehrmacht will forge forward until our blessed Führer's Reich is bigger than that of Alexander the Great."

Aunt Lydia smiled and nodded, but didn't add anything to the rant.

Herr Keller continued, "From North Sea to the Mediterranean, from the Atlantic Ocean to the Pacific Ocean, it will be one Grand German Reich. Heil Hitler!" Herr Keller jumped to his feet, his hand stretching forward in the obligatory *Hitlergruß*.

Everyone else in the room followed suit, and only Lotte skipped it because she had both hands full with the tray. The picture was ridiculous. Herr Keller, his wife, and son stood facing Lotte with their immaculate posture. In comparison, her aunt and cousins looked like peasants scattered on a chessboard, half-heartedly raising their right arms into the air.

Lotte focused on handing out the refreshments, or she would have laughed out loud. She couldn't stay here and listen to this another second. "Aunt Lydia, may I be excused? I forgot I still need to water the garden."

"Of course, Lotte." Lydia turned back to the mayor and his wife. "It's been such a blessing to have my niece with me. She helps with the chores and the little ones."

I wouldn't have to help if people like you hadn't sent all the grown men to war. I wouldn't even have to be here. I would be back home with my family.

Lotte stuck out her tongue while she slipped out the door and headed for the garden and the well. The sound of the door opening and shutting again made her turn around, and her heart sank.

"Go back inside, Hans," she said and hurried to the small shed, retrieving the watering can. But when she turned to leave, she found the doorway blocked by his large frame. She sighed. "I need to get the garden watered, and you're in my way."

Hans grinned. "Give me a kiss, and I'll let you pass."

Lotte hid her revulsion at the suggestion and picked up a shovel. "Let me pass, or I'll hit you with this."

"Oh, yeah?" He laughed, pulling the shovel from her hands. "Now, what are you going to do?"

Anger mixed with fear, and Lotte's eyes darted between Hans' strong body and the door. There was no way she could slip through. Goosebumps rose on her arms when she realized she was trapped.

Hans was still smiling when he moved forward, but nevertheless, he scared the hell out of her. With only a few feet between her back and the wall, she didn't have many options either. "Hans, move out of the way."

"I don't think I will." He put his hands on her shoulders, and she stiffened, helpless to prevent being pulled against him.

"Don't play difficult to get." He breathed into her ear. "You've been teasing me the entire school year."

Lotte shook her head in confusion. Despite attending the same class, she hadn't exchanged more than a few words with him in two years.

"That's better." Hans lowered his head and kissed her.

Lotte was too surprised to turn her face away in time, and his hands captured her head like a vise. She pressed her lips together and pushed her hands against his chest, but several long moments passed before he moved back.

"Now, that was nice. Wasn't it?" he said, licking his lips.

Lotte's vision filled with red, and she slapped him across the face as hard as she could. He looked shocked and rubbed his cheek before spitting on the ground. "You're going to regret that."

"Oh yes? What are you going to do? I promise I'll slap you even harder if you lay hands on me ever again."

Hans dropped his hands, and lowered his voice. "I won't have to do anything. My father is the mayor and the chief of police. He could take your aunt's farm away from her if he wanted to. One word from me is all it would take."

Even as he finished his threat, he took another step towards her and Lotte's entire being filled with horror. But Hans didn't try to touch her again.

"Think about your aunt next time you plan to deny me what I want." The threat in his voice lingered long after he had left the shed and returned to the house.

As soon as Hans was out of sight, Lotte crumpled to the ground, wrapping her arms around her middle.

CHAPTER 8

Lotte spent a restless night in her room. Hans had given her quite a fright when he stole a kiss from her, but that was nothing compared to the terror seeping into her bones when she thought of his father and what he was capable of.

Would Herr Keller really take Aunt Lydia's farm away? The same way he'd done with the Epstein farm? An even more terrifying thought entered her mind. *What if he sends Aunt Lydia away because of me? What will happen to my cousins?*

Rage boiled in her blood at the injustice. Hans was the one in the wrong. He had taken liberties he had no right to take.

After a long night of little sleep, she grabbed her bicycle and pedaled to Mindelheim to visit with Irmhild. Lotte caught her getting ready to leave the house.

"What are you doing here this early?" Irmhild asked and braided her long hair skillfully into a crown around her head.

"Hans. He trapped me in the shed and stole a kiss."

"Hans is vile." Irmhild wrinkled her nose as she tucked a few daisies into her braids. "Handsome, but he doesn't know how to treat girls."

"He threatened to have his dad take my aunt's farm," Lotte cried, tears flowing down her cheeks.

Irmhild hugged her tight. "I'm afraid that isn't an idle threat. Hans is bad enough. There are rumors about how he treats girls. He's not a nice boy."

"Tell me about it." Lotte used her fingers to dry her tears.

"But his father..." Irmhild paused, giving her a serious look. "His father is even worse. He's my boss, and I've witnessed the many times he hasn't shown an ounce of compassion at all. He might as well climb over dead bodies."

"So, what? Hans can kiss me whenever he wishes? Is that the glorious Nazi life?" Rage rose in Lotte's veins again.

"Of course he doesn't have the right to kiss you against your will, but...well, hear me out for a minute, will you?"

Lotte nodded, her face still an enraged mask.

"I mean...if all Hans wants are a couple of kisses, and it will keep your aunt from getting into trouble..." She lifted a shoulder. "Well, maybe letting him kiss you is the lesser of the two evils."

"I can't believe you just said that!" Lotte paced Irmhild's small room. "Besides, I can't have Nazis like Hans wandering around the farm, they'd find Ra–" Lotte froze in place as the original reason she'd needed to see her friend popped into her mind. "Enough about me, we have a bigger problem."

"We do?"

"Yes. I gave Rachel the papers, and she was overjoyed, but now where does she go?"

"What do you mean? She goes someplace safe." Irmhild had barely finished her sentence when her face fell. "Oh goodness, we haven't thought about that."

"I know. I feel stupid, but they can't just walk out of the barn. Everyone around here knows them."

"They could go to Munich," Irmhild suggested. Munich was the biggest city in Bavaria and only a two-hour train ride away.

"And do what?"

"I don't know. Surely Rachel can think of something." Irmhild put on her shoes and picked up her handbag. "I have to run some errands for my mom. Come with me?"

"Munich is being bombed by the enemy. People are leaving the city, not going there." Lotte linked arms with Irmhild and they left the house.

"You're right. What if we find them an abandoned house to stay in?" Irmhild suggested. "There are quite a few around."

"And how are they supposed to eat?" Lotte questioned.

"Well, they could apply for ration cards, just like everyone else."

"Again, they would have to go someplace where they weren't recognized, but where? And how do they get there?"

Irmhild shook her head. "Well, they can't take the train. They'd need to have travel permits, and that means coming into my office, and my supervisor will recognize them for sure. He'll also know that their papers are fake and then we'll all be in trouble."

The two girls grew quiet, the enormity of Rachel's situation weighing heavily on them.

"I've got it! You remember that convent near Kaufbeuren? It's just twenty miles away. They could go there."

Lotte raised a brow. "The convent? Do you know someone there?"

"Not me, but Uwe does. His aunt is a nun there."

Lotte gave her a hesitant look. "He's a friend of Hans. Can we trust him?"

"He's nothing like Hans, and we won't tell him the truth anyway. Besides, he fancies you. Ask him nicely, and I'm sure he'll help us to contact his aunt."

Lotte thought for a moment and then nodded. "Uwe sounds like our best option."

CHAPTER 9

"Don't you have to go to work today?" Lotte asked while Irmhild delivered several letters for her mother.

"Yes, but only half the day. I'm not due at the town hall until afternoon. I wouldn't want to draw undue attention to myself."

"Good. Where do you think Uwe could be?" They had returned to Irmhild's house and fetched their bicycles.

"Let's start at his place," Irmhild suggested.

"You know where he lives?"

"Sure I do. Follow me." Irmhild laughed. "Growing up here I know everyone and everything. It's not that big of a place."

Uwe wasn't at home, but his mother directed them to the patch of forest he was currently working in.

Lotte pedaled away, over rough and smooth until they reached the heavy copse of trees. She paused at the edge and waited for a breathless Irmhild to catch up.

"I guess we have to walk from here."

The girls parked their bikes by the side of the trail, not bothering to lock them, and followed the trail into the dense forest. It wasn't long before they heard the sound of an axe chopping wood and Irmhild pointed to their left. "That has to be him. No one else is allowed in here to cut down trees. Remember, be extra nice to him."

Lotte made a face but nodded and followed in the direction of the noise. A loud crash sounded, startling them both, and then silence settled over the forest once more.

"What was that?" Lotte asked.

"A falling tree. Uwe first fells the tree and then chops up the branches for firewood. Later, the trunks are pulled out and taken to the lumber mill."

"I had no idea. Does he do all of this by himself?" Lotte's admiration for Uwe grew.

"No, silly, of course not. He has an ox to pull the trunks to the edge of the forest where a tractor is waiting for them."

"Oh."

A few minutes later, the two girls stepped into a small clearing and stopped. Uwe was stripped to the waist, swinging his axe at the newly fallen tree, but when he saw them approaching, he stopped, a silly grin spreading across his face.

Irmhild gave Lotte a push, and she walked over toward him.

"Hi, Uwe," she greeted him, trying to figure out how to best broach the reason for her visit.

Uwe put down the axe and his eyes played over her face. "What brings you deep into the forest?"

"Looking for you," she answered honestly.

"Me?" The silly grin on his face intensified and he stood a little taller.

That was when Lotte noticed he wasn't wearing a shirt. His stomach and chest were nothing but muscles and showed a healthy tan. She couldn't tear her eyes away from his bulging biceps and followed his arms down to the strong hands that held the axe in place.

The tingles she felt in her body were a novel and confusing experience, as she'd never felt this kind of attraction to a man before. And she'd never seen Uwe as anything but a nice boy who happened to attend the same school. Until now.

Uwe seemed to be equally infatuated, his eyes wandering up and down her body until the sound of Irmhild clearing her throat broke the spell.

"So, you found me."

"We did. So…how have you been?" She couldn't have said anything sillier, but for some strange reason, her mind was blank.

The smile slid off his handsome face, and he made a violent gesture with his hand. "I've been drafted!"

Lotte gasped, her hands flying to her mouth.

"I'm sorry," Irmhild said, looking equally shaken.

"Yes? Well, so am I. I have to report next month, the day after I turn seventeen." His face took on a desperate expression. "Damn war. I thought being the forest warden would save me. But evidently, it hasn't."

"But hasn't the *Hitlerjugend* trained you to be a soldier already?" Lotte asked.

"Pah. Everyone has to join the *Hitlerjugend,* but that

doesn't mean I want to fight and kill." He sank down on the trunk, dropping the axe to the ground.

"So why hasn't Hans been drafted? He's already turned eighteen." Lotte threw a hand over her mouth, but it was already too late, and the words had been uttered.

"That's what makes this all the more maddening. Hans should have been drafted a year ago, but his father is the chief of police and the boss of the Party. I doubt he'll ever join the lowly soldiers' ranks."

"That's not fair." Lotte sat beside him on the trunk with compassion in her heart. She hated injustice, and the entire Nazi regime was one big inequity.

"Life is never fair," Uwe sneered before raising his impossibly blue eyes to Lotte. "So, tell me why you came all the way out here to find me."

Again, Lotte's mind blanked.

"Well, Lotte asked me if I knew anyone who was a nun, and I remembered you have an aunt who is one." Irmhild came to her rescue.

"You want to talk to a nun? Whatever for?"

"I'd rather not say. Does your aunt live close?" Lotte looked down at her hands.

"Yes, you could get there on that bicycle I always see you riding. She lives in a convent about twenty miles from here." A worried look flashed across his handsome face. "You're not thinking of becoming a nun, are you?"

"Maybe. But I have some questions and didn't know who to ask." She hated lying to him, but she still wasn't sure whether she could trust him or not.

Uwe gave her a critical look and then grinned. "Fine. I'll take you to see my aunt, but I'm not buying that you want to become a nun. Not even for a minute." He rolled his neck and nodded to the tree he'd been cutting branches from. "I should get back to work. When do you want to go?"

"Could we go tomorrow?"

"Sure. We'll have to go early, it's a long ride. Is six o'clock at the fountain alright?"

"I'll be there." Lotte wanted to hug him but simply smiled at him instead. "Thank you so much."

CHAPTER 10

The next day, Lotte got up well before dawn, took care of her morning chores, and left a note for her aunt, telling her she needed to help Irmhild with something in the next town. She'd done this same thing so many times, she wasn't concerned about her aunt's being worried or upset.

Dressed in her new dress and plimsolls, she arrived at the fountain just in time. Uwe was already waiting for her, an immense black bicycle by his side.

"Thanks for doing this for me." She greeted him with a shy smile.

"No problem. You look very nice in that dress."

Lotte felt the blood rushing to her cheeks. "Thanks, my mother made it for me."

"Let's go. Twenty miles is a long way to ride. Are you sure you're up for it?"

For a moment Lotte wanted to tell him that she was very capable of riding double or even triple the distance, but the caring look in his eyes confused her enough to swallow her spiteful remark. "I'm ready to go."

They rode for a while in silence, as the sun rose over the horizon, showing clear blue skies. Night chill lingered in the air, but the day would be hot again. The wheat, rye, and barley fields lay harvested, but the cornfields stood strong and tall, reminding her of the imminent harvest. The sooner Rachel and her siblings left the barn, the better it would be for everyone.

After about an hour, they heard the sounds of an aircraft approaching.

"Off into the bushes," Uwe shouted. He jumped off his bicycle and pushed it into the roadside ditch. Then he took Lotte's hand and pulled her with him to seek cover beneath a row of bushes.

Despite the danger looming in the air, all she sensed was his intense presence, the way he took care of the situation and made her feel safe.

"Bloody Englishmen." Uwe pointed to where two aircraft were hanging low in the sky, as if in search of something. Usually, the bombers didn't bother with the countryside and preferred to drop their deadly cargo over the big cities, but one could never be sure.

Lotte shuddered as memories of the air raids in Berlin swam in her brain.

"Are you cold?" Uwe asked.

"No, it's just..." She didn't know how to finish her sentence.

"Just what?" His voice became softer than she'd ever heard it before.

"Those aircraft reminded me of the raid when I was in

Berlin." She shuddered again. "My sister saved me. I was too scared to run. Ursula had to return and drag me out of the building all the way to the shelter."

"Did she often have to rescue you?"

"Often?" Lotte scrunched her nose.

"I mean when you were younger."

"Actually, no." Lotte smiled, caught up in her memories. "Ursula has never done anything wrong in her life. She always behaved the way she was expected to and never got herself into trouble."

"Doesn't sound like you're related." Uwe grinned.

Lotte laughed at his remark. Attending the same school, he had witnessed firsthand her lack of obedience. She'd frequently been the recipient of thwacks from their teacher. "No, as children she rarely covered up for me. I guess she thought I deserved my punishment for stepping out of line."

"You never told me why you're living with your aunt."

"That's a long story." Lotte sighed. She still didn't trust him enough to tell him that she'd been expelled from the *Bund Deutscher Mädel* for speaking against the Nazis. Nor that her sharp tongue and rash actions had drawn unwanted attention. "Let's just say my parents thought it would be safer for me out here in the sticks."

Uwe squinted his eyes at her but didn't press the point. Long after the planes had vanished from their sight, he finally declared it safe to get on their bicycles again. Twice more, they were forced to hide in the bushes or trees along the side of the road to avoid detection.

"That plane was flying a lot closer to the ground," Uwe said as they got back on the bikes for the third time.

"Are we almost there?" she asked.

"A few more miles." He gave her a teasing wink. "Tired already?"

"Not a chance." She grinned and pedaled hard until her heart was thundering in her chest. But every time she attempted to pass him, he shook his head, grinned, and went just fast enough to keep her at bay. It was infuriating, but at the same time it was incredible fun, and it kept her mind from worrying about the aircraft.

An hour later, they were standing in front of the convent doors. Lotte's face was hot from the exercise, and she didn't doubt her mane was in wild curls around her head. She tried combing it with her fingers until she noticed Uwe's gaze on her.

"What's the matter?"

"I like your hair. It fits your personality."

Her face grew even hotter. "Aww…thanks."

His blue eyes fixed on hers, and she squirmed under his scrutiny. "Care to tell me why you really want to speak to my aunt?" Uwe asked.

Lotte frowned at him. Irmhild had impressed on her that she couldn't tell a soul. Ever. As much as she hated lying to Uwe, it was for the best. "I did tell you. I'm thinking of joining a convent and had some questions only a nun could answer."

Uwe opened his mouth to argue, but in that very moment, the door opened, and an elderly nun stepped out, her black habit flowing behind her.

"Good morning, Sister." Lotte gave her a tentative smile.

"Good morning. What can we do for you?" she answered, not unfriendly.

Uwe stepped forward. "My aunt is a nun here, and my friend would like to speak with her."

"What is your aunt's name?"

"Gretchen…I mean Sister Margarete."

The nun nodded and opened the door wider, addressing Uwe. "Only women are allowed inside these walls. You will have to wait outside." Then she turned to Lotte. "What is your name?"

"Charlotte Klausen." Her insides trembled, and Lotte, despite not being particularly religious, sent a quick prayer to heaven. *Please, God, let these nuns receive Rachel and her siblings.*

"Follow me," the nun said.

Lotte stepped inside, and as soon as the door clicked shut, she felt the sudden urge to bolt. The atmosphere in the convent was so different from the outside. Quiet, sublime, but also eerie. She followed the nun through long and dark corridors until she was ushered into a small room with a table and several chairs.

"Please sit and wait. I'll find Sister Margarete for you." The nun disappeared, leaving her alone in the creepy room.

Lotte hadn't thought out what exactly to tell the nun and wished Uwe was by her side. But on the other hand, it was easier to talk to his aunt in private.

The temperature inside the thick walls of the convent was chilly compared to outside. Right now, it was a welcome refresher, but Lotte thought it must be uncomfortable in winter time. She glanced at the crucifix hanging on the wall. According to Aunt Lydia, before Hitler's seizure of power, there'd been crucifixes in most buildings in Bavaria. Schools, town halls, private homes, everyone proudly displayed their affiliation with the Catholic religion. Until the swastikas and Hitler portraits replaced them.

Even in tiny villages like Kleindorf, National Socialism brought everyone into line, seeping into every corner of the people's lives. At school, they learned about the Aryan Master Race. The *Hitlerjugend* prepared boys for war. The *Bund Deutscher Mädel* hammered the ideal of the submissive wife into the girls. Couples were given a copy of Hitler's *Mein Kampf* for their wedding. People who didn't attend the monthly Party meeting were frowned upon. Even the farmer's association promoted the greatness of Hitler's Reich first and agriculture-related topics second.

The door creaked open, jolting Lotte from her thoughts.

"Good morning. I'm Sister Margarete." The nun wore the same black habit as the first, but her face looked much younger and softer.

Lotte curtsied. "Nice to meet you, Sister."

"They tell me my nephew brought you here. How is he?" Sister Margarete asked softly.

"Uwe is fine. He's doing his father's work as a forest warden." Lotte paused for a moment. She wasn't sure whether she should worry the nun with his imminent departure to the front lines.

"He's such a good chap. He's always been my favorite nephew. But now, tell me, what can I do for you?"

Lotte squirmed. "It's an unusual request."

"Nothing is unusual before the eyes of God," the nun answered. "Please tell me why you took the long journey to our convent."

"It's..." She paused, hoping to be forgiven for bending the truth a bit. "I found four orphans, and they are currently staying on my aunt's farm, but my aunt has five, soon six, children of her own to feed, seven with me. She can't possibly care for them as well."

"Usually, the authorities ask us to accept orphans into the orphanage, but in this case, I would have to ask the Reverend Mother if she will make an exception for your foundlings."

The expression on Sister Margarete's face resembled Uwe's expression when he hadn't believed her excuse. Lotte fidgeted with her hands, fully expecting the nun to insist on more information. But no words left the nun's lips.

"Please? They have Aryan papers, if that helps."

Sister Margarete raised her eyebrow at this. "I will see if the Reverend Mother has time for me to speak with her now. Please wait here."

Sister Margarete left the room as quietly as she'd entered. Lotte leaned back in the hard wooden chair and tried to get control over the slight tremble in her body. Nothing bad had happened, and she hadn't even lied. She'd just left out some crucial information.

An eternity later, Sister Margarete returned. "Reverend Mother has agreed that the four orphans may come here. Since the war started, many children have found themselves in need of our care."

Lotte expected her to ask more questions, but she didn't. The nuns probably thought it was best not to know too much.

"Come, I will see you out and speak with my nephew for a moment." Sister Margarete led her toward the doors to the convent and spoke quietly with Uwe for quite some time.

When the church bells tolled, she bowed her head and went back inside.

"Did my aunt answer your questions?" Uwe asked, full of curiosity.

Lotte grinned at his badly concealed attempt to extract more information from her. "She did. Thank you again for bringing me here."

"We should return home. It's starting to get hot."

Lotte's stomach grumbled, and she remembered that in her anxiety to get to the convent, she'd forgotten to pack lunch. Sister Margarete had offered her water but nothing to eat.

"Hungry?" Uwe asked.

"Like a wolf, but I forgot to bring any food."

"Good that you have me, I'm willing to share." He pointed toward the bag on his rear rack. "Let's ride until we find a nice spot to sit down and eat."

They found a meadow with fruit trees to give them shade and a small creek lazily flowing along. Both of them took off their shoes and dangled their feet into the cool and clear water while eating the sandwiches he brought.

He refilled his bottle with fresh water from the creek and handed it to Lotte. His smile – and the dimples that appeared every time he laughed – did funny things to her insides. She quickly looked away and emptied the bottle.

Standing with both feet in the cool water, Lotte refilled the bottle and handed it to him. For a moment, their hands touched, and something even stranger happened. It was as if she'd touched an electric fence, but stronger, the sensation rippling in waves throughout her entire body. She moved a step away from him and sat down on the grass again. When

Uwe finished drinking, he glanced at her as if he saw her for the first time.

"So, why did you really want to go to the convent?" Uwe asked with a disarming smile. "And don't tell me you want to become a nun. You're not the type to sequester yourself away for the rest of your life. You can't even keep silent for five minutes."

"Very well, I don't want to become a nun. It sounds really boring." Lotte bit her bottom lip, racking her brain over how much to tell him.

"So why lie to me?" Uwe leaned back on his elbows and scrutinized her face.

Her temper immediately flared. "I didn't lie! I simply chose not to tell you everything."

"That's how it's called nowadays? Not telling everything." His tone was teasing, but she could sense the underlying hurt.

She exhaled a deep breath before meeting his eyes again. "I didn't know if I could trust you."

"So, do you trust me now?"

"I'm not sure," Lotte answered truthfully, without thinking. The hurt look in his beautiful blue eyes slashed her heart, and she wanted to make up for her lapse. "Look. It's not that I don't like you…I mean…for God's sake…" She broke off and looked across the meadow onto the road.

Her instinct told her that he wouldn't betray her, but Irmhild had hammered the need for secrecy into Lotte's brain so many times she didn't want to disappoint her. They weren't simply two girls anymore but future war heroes, spies on a mission. And as such, one had to be secretive. Everyone knew that.

"Are you…in a delicate condition?" Uwe asked with a low voice.

It took Lotte a few moments to grasp the meaning, but then she flushed furiously, her cheeks probably matching the flaming color of her hair. "Of course not. I'm not that kind of girl! I found four orphans living in the woods a few days ago."

"Who is it?" he asked, ignoring her mortification.

"Their last name is Müller. They're just children, and I needed to find a safe place for them to stay. They can't keep sleeping in my aunt's barn." She slapped her hand across her mouth, groaning at her stupidity.

"I see."

"Yes. Don't be mad, but I wasn't sure if you'd help me if I told you the real reason I wanted to go to the convent."

Uwe got to his feet. "We should get going. We still have another two hours to ride."

When they arrived at Mindelheim, Lotte tried to think of some way to thank him, but nothing came to mind. Uwe rode up next to her and then reached over and touched her hand. "I had a good time with you."

It took a long time for the new spark of electricity to fade.

CHAPTER 11

Lotte arrived home just in time to complete her evening chores – except for milking the cows – with no time to look for Rachel. She was bursting with the need to spread the good news and had to bite her tongue many times during dinner to not tell Aunt Lydia.

She'd already told Uwe too much, despite her good intentions to keep her lips sealed. This wouldn't happen again, she promised herself. After dinner, she stayed in the kitchen to help clear the dishes, every single fiber in her body aching to dash to the barn. Seconds dragged into minutes, and when everything was finally cleared up, she took to her heels.

In the barn, Rachel and her siblings were anxiously waiting for her in the loft.

"Lotte! I was worried about you. What did Irmhild say?" Rachel asked.

"I have wonderful news." Lotte cast a triumphant smile and rose to her full height of five feet seven. "There's a

Catholic convent that will accept the four of you in their orphanage."

She hadn't even finished pronouncing the word *orphanage* when little Mindel screamed, "We're no orphans! We need no orphan place! I want to go home!"

Rachel's shoulders sagged, a petrified expression on her face as she quickly shushed her little sister. "Sweetie, don't cry. Remember we're playing hide and seek? Nobody can know we're here."

Mindel did her best to dry her tears but continued to sob in a low voice while her two older brothers exchanged glances, clearly indicating they didn't buy into the hide-and-seek game. They had the bodies of elementary school lads, but their eyes showed the knowing look of adults. Lotte's heart squeezed.

"Will we get food from the nuns?" Aron asked.

"There will be plenty of food," Lotte reassured him, but she barely managed not to break into tears herself. The past few years had been brutal on everyone, but just how much more had these children suffered? Mockery. Ostracism. Hunger. And now the loss of their parents and their home.

She took Rachel aside so the others couldn't hear. "The sooner you leave, the better. Wait until all the lights in the main house are turned off, and then go."

"How far is it?" Rachel asked.

"Twenty miles. You know the convent in Kaufbeuren, right?"

Rachel nodded.

"I know it seems like a long way, but during the night, you can walk on the road, and no one will bother you. You should be able to reach the convent at daybreak."

"Mindel will never be able to walk that far. I'll have to carry her most of the way," Rachel murmured.

Lotte wanted to offer her bicycle, but that would cause plenty of questions. "You should be fine by the time you have passed the neighboring villages. Beyond that, nobody will know you. And with your papers, you're just another group of children seeking refuge."

"I have been to Kaufbeuren before and know where the convent is. I can't thank you enough, Lotte." Rachel hugged her, tears of gratitude in her eyes. "Thank you so much."

"I'm glad I could help. Please be safe and live a happy life. Maybe you can send me a postcard once the war is over?" Lotte released herself from the embrace and climbed down the ladder to milk the cows.

It was already dark by the time she finished milking the last one, and exhaustion pulled at her. She strained the milk and then sent a final look and well wishes back into the barn. *Go with Godspeed!*

Then she returned to the house, carefully navigating in the darkness. She rounded the hedge, her eyes fixed on the lit windows when someone stepped out of the shadows and into her path.

"Ah!" she screamed in fright. "Who's there?"

A moment later, she recognized Hans blocking her way. Her heart sank to her knees. *Goodness, I hope he's not here to demand another kiss.* Gathering up all her courage, she said, "Hans, you scared me."

"Did I?" Hans sneered at her and took a step forward, whispering into her ear, "I told you that you would regret not being nice to me." When he stepped aside, she noticed two more men standing behind him, and even more beyond.

"Uwe, is that you? What are you doing here?" Her voice almost broke with fear. The way Uwe stood, looking as if he wished to be anywhere but here, caused her breath to catch in her throat. Her eyes darted to the big person taking a step toward her, and she recognized Hans' father. His menacing stance made one thing clear: this wasn't a social call.

Her eyes returned to Uwe, silently begging him for help, but he looked away.

Traitor! Miserable piece of scum.

"Fräulein Klausen, I was informed that suspicious things are happening on this farm and I'm here to get to the nub of the matter."

Lotte trembled with fury and fear, but before she could say anything, Herr Keller shoved her aside and started walking up the same path she'd just come down, several of his minions joining him as they searched the barn. Hans and Uwe followed. Lotte wanted to run into the house and hide her head under a pillow, but to what avail? Maybe she could talk the mayor into letting the Epstein children go?

Some ten minutes later, Herr Keller and the other men exited the barn dragging the four children between them. Loud cries filled the air, but after one of the men slapped Rachel and threatened to shoot them there and then, the screams quieted down to small whimpers.

There was nothing Lotte could do but watch in horror as the four children were dragged away, talk of deportation and filthy Jews filling the air. Uwe appeared by her side, giving her an apologetic glance. But apart from that small gesture, he did nothing but stand by and watch.

Filthy coward.

When Hans returned with a disgusting grin, Lotte couldn't keep her rage at bay for one moment longer. "You bastard. It's all your fault. Sending innocent children away!" She raised her fists, drumming them against his chest. He caught her hands with a dirty chuckle and held them high over her head. Lotte struggled. "You...you filthy...wimp. You aren't even man enough to go off to war. Everyone in our class got drafted, but not you. What did your hideous father do, pull some special strings to keep Mummy's darling at home?"

A hard slap to her face ended Lotte's rant. She rubbed her cheek and stared in shock at Hans' father, who'd probably heard her entire tirade.

"Watch your mouth," he growled.

"You have no right to treat me like this," she spat at him.

"Actually, I do," the mayor answered. "Wait and see." Then he turned to his son. "Bring her along as well."

Hans caught her around the waist and threw her over his shoulder like a sack of flour, and despite Lotte's kicking, punching, and scratching, he carried her towards the police automobile parked in front of her aunt's house.

"You can't take me away. I haven't done anything!" she screamed in the faint hope that someone – anyone – would come to her rescue.

"I'm arresting you just because I can," the mayor said. "I hope it will prove a valuable lesson to you."

Valuable lesson? Damn Nazi vermin. For once, she managed to keep her mouth shut, struggling in earnest to free herself from Hans' grip. But the more she struggled, the tighter he held her, his grip growing stronger until she could barely breathe.

"I warned you, *Schätzchen,*" Hans whispered in her ear before shoving her into the back seat.

Lotte thought she caught a glimpse of a shadow in one of the upstairs windows, but she couldn't be sure. Even if Aunt Lydia had seen her, what could she do? Lotte was too angry to cry, but she knew the tears would come later.

CHAPTER 12

The police station in Mindelheim possessed only one holding cell, for which Lotte was grateful. At least she wasn't alone in the dank, dirty cell with bars on the windows and door.

As miserable as her situation was, at least she shared it with Rachel and her siblings. Lotte sank to the floor, her arms around her legs, her head hidden between her knees. She didn't want to see or hear anything. Not the threadbare woolen blankets lying on the single cot. Not the moss growing in the cracks on the wall. And definitely not Rachel's quiet but desperate voice trying to comfort her younger brothers and sister.

Rachel had given each of them a blanket and was now talking Mindel and Aron into lying down to sleep. So far, it wasn't working, and Lotte couldn't blame them. She raised her head and looked through the iron bars into the hallway. The cell was located in the basement of the police station, with no sounds coming through the thick ceiling.

This is all my fault. I should never have trusted Uwe, she scolded herself, sniffling to hold back her tears. Crying wouldn't do anyone any good, and she didn't want to scare the children even more. Lost in thought, she started at the sound of the heavy iron door leading upstairs opening and closing, then footsteps coming down the hall. Instinctively, she crouched closer against the wall.

Hans appeared on the other side of the iron bars. Despite hating him with a passion, she felt a sliver of relief that it wasn't his father or one of the Nazi officers.

"Not so high and mighty now, are we?" he sneered at her.

"Hans, there's been a terrible mistake. Please help us get out of here."

He shook his head and took a step toward her. "It's too much fun to see you suffering for what you've done to me."

"I haven't done anything," she burst out.

"Well, you humiliated me in front of my father." Hans grimaced and gestured for her to come to the bars.

Lotte hesitated but then obeyed. It wouldn't do any good to infuriate him any more. When they stood facing each other, only separated by metal bars, he said, "Do you know what they do to traitors? All of those awful rumors the teachers told us not to believe…well, they're true. You're going to get a chance to experience them firsthand. Unless…"

Lotte wrapped her arms around her midriff, trying to keep the images away that were storming her mind. Medical experiments gone awry, hangings, torture, and human beings treated worse than animals. A violent shudder shook her body, and she had to grab the metal bars with both hands to steady herself. She closed her eyes to fight the bile rising in her throat. After several deep inhalations, she opened her eyes again to see that Hans had unlocked the cell door and slipped in beside her.

"Hans?"

"It doesn't have to be like this, you know?" He pushed her against the stone wall and caged her in, putting his palms against the wall on either side of her head and moving his body in so close that she touched his chest with each breath she took.

Lotte thinned her lips to stop from screaming and tried to move away from him, but he buried a hand in her hair and held her in place.

"Let me go," Lotte begged.

"You want your freedom? I can make it happen. You just have to be nice to me." Hans looked over his shoulder where Rachel stood, protecting her younger siblings from witnessing the scene. "You, come over here," he demanded.

Rachel shuffled across the small cell. Hans reached out and grabbed her breast when she was close enough, causing Rachel to cry out in alarm and revulsion. Lotte pushed against him. "Let go of her! You have no right to molest her."

Hans laughed and squeezed Rachel's breast again before ripping her dress down the front. "Let's see what goods you have to offer. Maybe I can convince my father to go easier on you as well."

When Rachel tried to back up, he said in a low voice, "Stand still, or maybe you'd rather I amuse myself with one of them?" He nodded towards her siblings, who were huddled together in the corner, trying not to make any noise as tears streamed down their faces.

Red-hot rage coiled in Lotte's veins, and she attacked him with all her strength. He let go of Rachel and turned his attention to her. His half-amused expression vanished when she spat in his face.

Hans raised his hand and slapped her across the face so hard, she fell to the floor.

Lotte clasped her cheek, tasting blood as it trickled from the corner of her mouth. Her head was spinning, her eyes watering, and she watched helplessly as Hans took a threatening step towards her.

"Hans! Get out of there!" Herr Keller barked.

"Rot in hell, Lotte!" Hans kicked at her before he slammed out of the cell and pulled the door shut.

Lotte pushed herself to sit, expecting the mayor to scold his son.

"You're nothing but trash. A dog deserves better treatment than you do," Herr Keller lashed out at her with a crimson face. "*Judenfreund*. I wouldn't be surprised if you were a Jew yourself."

Lotte shook her head in disbelief.

"I'll investigate that point, and if I find any Jewish blood in you or your aunt, she and her brood will be joining the rest of the scum on one of the deportation trains." Herr Keller turned to Hans. "Get on home and leave this filth alone."

They left, leaving their prisoners in the dark, the only sliver of light coming from the moon through the bars on the window. Lotte was shivering when Rachel slipped an arm around her and led her over to the cot.

"I'm so sorry," Lotte murmured. "I didn't want to cause any harm to my aunt or cousins. I just wanted to help."

"It's not your fault." Rachel hugged her tight. Two frightened girls in a dark cell.

But it is. Everything's my fault. For acting rashly and opening my stupid mouth before thinking. How often has Mutter warned me?

"I should have let Hans have his way…" she whispered into the dark. "Maybe if I'd let him kiss me…told him he's a nice fellow but I'm too young to do more than hold hands. I should have sweet talked him instead of punching him."

"Stop it," Rachel said. "It's no use blaming yourself for what happened. It just makes things worse."

A little body snuggled up against Lotte, and she lifted Mindel onto her lap. The little girl pressed against her chest, wrapping her arms around her for warmth. Lotte looked over to see Rachel doing the same with Aron. Ten-year-old Israel laid his head in her lap, and Rachel occasionally ran her fingers through his hair in a comforting gesture.

When all three children were finally asleep, Rachel looked at Lotte with tears in her eyes. "What will happen to us? And to you?"

"I don't know," Lotte whispered, her tears breaking all dams and rushing down her face. They both sat on the cote, their backs leaned against the wall, their shoulders touching, seeking the comfort of being close to another person. They stayed like that as the hours slipped away, neither of them sleeping or talking, simply sitting in silence.

Sometime in the wee hours of the morning, Lotte started as the sound of steps walking towards their cell reached her ears. She nudged Rachel and pointed towards the door, her eyes straining in the darkness to see who was there.

When a light illuminated Uwe's face, Lotte opened her mouth to scream at him, but he put a finger to his lips and whispered, "Shush. I'm here to get you out."

Lotte was stunned into silence and stared at him bug-eyed as he unlocked the cell door and then stepped inside, relieving Lotte of the sleeping child on her lap.

"Don't just sit there. Let's go," Uwe whispered, nudging her to stand up. The touch of his fingers on her upper arm sent life back into her body – and shame.

Rachel woke up her brothers, and they followed Uwe upstairs to the police station, where he carefully hung the cell keys on their hook again. Then they snuck out the front door, ducking into the shadows of the night, becoming one with the wall of the building.

Uwe motioned for them to follow him and led them across the harvested fields to the edge of the woods, carrying sleeping Mindel. Except for the shuffling of feet, they made no sound, barely daring to breathe.

Once they reached the road leading to Kaufbeuren, he stopped and set Mindel down. Only half awake, she clung to Rachel's leg. Uwe pointed south. "Go. All of you. As fast as you can and don't stop until you've reached the convent."

"Uwe…" Rachel said, but he shook his head and stepped back.

"You have to hot foot it."

Lotte's faced burned with shame for how wrong she'd pegged him, and for how thoroughly she'd messed up. If it weren't for her rash, self-righteous behavior, Hans would never have started his personal vendetta against her and caught the Jewish children in the process. It was about time she put the needs of others before hers.

"Uwe. I can never thank you enough for what you did, but I cannot go to the convent. The mayor will be looking for me, and since I don't have fake papers like the others do, I would only endanger them."

Uwe looked at her for a moment and then nodded in agreement. "Fine."

Lotte hugged Rachel, Aron, Israel, and Mindel one last time. "Good luck. Be safe."

"Thank you for everything. If God allows, we'll meet again after the war," Rachel said, tears falling from her eyes.

"Goodbye."

CHAPTER 13

Lotte watched them until they had disappeared in the dark and then turned to Uwe. "Now what?"

"Come with me," he answered and set off into the forest.

Lotte followed Uwe deeper and deeper into the trees, crawling up inclines or sliding down ravines, but constantly moving into foreign territory. She soon lost orientation, but every time fear snuck up on her, she glanced at Uwe's broad shoulders in front of her and felt safe. By now, her new birthday dress was covered in dirt, as were her plimsolls. They turned out to be a blessing, protecting her feet from the sticks and stones that littered the forest floor. Just when she wanted to drop down in exhaustion, Uwe stopped in front of a small hut in a clearing that Lotte had never seen before.

"Where are we?" she asked.

"Deep in the woods. No one but my father and I know about this place, so you should be safe here." His big hands hung loosely from his arms, his face a crooked smile.

He opened the door and lit a candle so that she could step inside. "It's the best I could come up with."

"It's perfect." Lotte smiled, although she was terrified at spending the night alone out here. Memories of the fairy tales her mother had read her when she was a child assaulted her brain. Hänsel and Gretel. Alone in the woods, tricked by the wicked witch. Snow White and the Seven Dwarfs. Persecuted by the evil stepmother.

Why is the villain in the fairy tales always a woman, when in real life we have to fear the men? Men like Hans, his father, the SS men, Hitler himself.

The sound of Uwe clearing his throat brought her back to the present.

"Thank you for everything, Uwe. I guess you should return before anyone realizes you're gone."

"I can't go back. Who do you think Herr Keller will blame for helping the prisoners escape? Not his men. They were too happy about their catch, talking about recognition and praise."

Hot and cold shivers ran down her spine as the momentousness of Uwe's sacrifice dawned on her.

"I…I didn't want to get anyone in hot water. It's all my fault." Tears started slipping from her eyes, but she stubbornly rubbed them off her face.

"It was my own choice. Nobody forced me to help you. Might as well get comfortable for the rest of the night."

A distinctive tension lingered between them, and for once, Lotte had no quick-witted answer. She looked around the small hut in the dim light of the candle. Huddled in the corner was a straw mattress. She laid it on the floor and plopped down, her hands around her legs, her head buried deep between her knees. Oh, how she wished to rewind time and make things right.

After a while, she sensed Uwe sitting down beside her. Close enough to feel the warmth of his body, but too far to touch.

"I'm sorry I didn't trust you."

"You thought I turned you in," he stated – not a question, just a fact.

"I didn't know what else to think when I saw you at my aunt's farm with Hans and his father." The mention of her aunt threatened to start her tears anew. She sniffed. "You were the only one who knew I'd found the orphans."

Uwe sighed. "Hans had been following you for a while already. I intercepted him and his father on their way to your aunt's farm and tagged along, hoping I could somehow warn you."

"I don't know that it would have made any difference. Rachel and her siblings were going to leave at midnight anyway."

A long silence ensued between them until Uwe spoke up again. "Hans had set his eyes on you, and every time you pushed him away, he became more determined to conquer you."

Lotte shivered at the memory of Hans' violent kisses. The way she'd felt defenseless and vulnerable in his steely grasp. Her eyes locked with Uwe's baby blue ones, sending electric tingles rushing through her body. She wondered what it would be like to be kissed by a boy she liked.

She didn't have to wonder for long. Uwe hesitantly reached out a hand to touch a loose curl, tucking it behind her ear. Instinctively, she leaned towards him until his hand cupped her chin.

"I want to kiss you," he said.

I want to kiss you too.

Lotte nodded and closed her eyes as his lips met hers. His lips were soft and accommodating, no more than a whiff of sweet touch. After a few seconds, they both drew back, the wonderment on his face mirroring her own emotions.

They settled back on the mattress, putting a few inches between themselves.

Uwe took several breaths and then murmured, "I'm a deserter now."

"But you weren't supposed to report for duty until the day after your birthday," Lotte objected.

"It won't matter. Apart from that, I'm also on the run for helping five prisoners escape."

Lotte reached out a hand to put it over his. "They were going to send Rachel and her siblings on a deportation train in the morning."

"I know. I overheard the mayor talking to Hans. I couldn't let that happen." He took a long breath. "My two older brothers died at the front. We have no news from my father…but whenever one of them was on furlough, their eyes would tell the truth. They never explicitly told me, but I put two and two together. After the *Wehrmacht* has occupied a town, the SS is sent in…" Uwe's voice creaked. "Having witnessed firsthand the cruelties Hans' father and his SS friends have committed, it wasn't difficult to imagine. I used to like the Nazis and thought Hitler was doing good things for Germany. That the war was a necessary evil, but now… I hate the atrocious things they do."

Lotte opened her mouth, but he anticipated her question and shook his head. "Don't ask because I won't tell you. The SS like to boast about the inhumane things they do. It makes me sick."

She nodded, and silence filled the small hut once again. After several long moments, she spoke quietly, "I'm sorry about your brothers. We haven't heard from either my father or my brother in almost a year. Nobody seems to know where they are, or if they are even still alive. For all I know, they might be prisoners of war in Russia."

"Is that where they were sent? The Russian front?" Uwe asked and wrapped an arm around her shoulders when she started to sob. "Shush, try to get some sleep. We'll figure things out in the morning. Close your eyes and rest."

Lotte believed she would never be able to sleep in her life again, but the security of his arm around her shoulders and his voice providing comfort soothed her into an exhausted slumber. Already dreaming, she sensed how he laid her down on the mattress and snuggled up beside her.

CHAPTER 14

Morning came, and Lotte woke with a stiff body. Late in September, the days were still warm, but the nights had become chilly. She glanced at her side and found Uwe murmuring in his sleep.

She tried to stretch without waking him but wasn't successful.

"Morning," he greeted her with a yawn.

Her grumbling stomach drowned out her reply.

"Hungry?" He propped himself on his elbow and glanced at her as if this was the first time he'd seen her.

"Starving." Lotte raised a hand to her curly hair, which refused to be tamed and probably looked like a wild mess atop her head. He chuckled, and Lotte felt self-consciousness rising. She'd never given a penny for her looks before.

"Good." Uwe smiled. "Let's see if we can find us some breakfast. Here, take this." He handed her a bucket and took another one for himself. He led her to a nearby creek, where they quenched their thirst and took a quick once over, refreshing themselves. Then they carried the buckets of water back to the hut and went in search of edible plants. In autumn, the forest blossomed with berries, mushrooms, nuts, and edible plants. For a few more weeks they would find enough food to survive.

"Shush," Uwe whispered. He froze. In the clearing ahead of them, several rabbits hopped around. Uwe produced a slingshot from his pocket and crouched down, one hand searching for a stone while his eyes stayed glued to the rabbits.

Whoooshhh. The stone flew through the air, and one of the rabbits fell to its side while the others scattered in panic.

"Gee. You're a good shot," Lotte said in awe.

A proud smile spread across Uwe's face. "Once learned, never forgotten. That's our dinner for tonight. Now we just need to find some dry wood. We'll need to be careful with the smoke, though. You know how to cook this critter?"

"I've only ever cooked chickens," she answered truthfully.

"Well, let's hope it works the same." He chuckled. "I can gut and skin it, but the cooking is above my pay grade."

Lotte watched him gutting the still warm animal and making short work of skinning it. When finished, he picked up the skin and the rabbit, and they returned to the hut, where he started a fire in the pit. Everything he did looked so easy, so normal.

Meanwhile, she searched for something they could use as a pot, but apart from the two metal buckets, there wasn't anything of use.

"I guess we'd better grill our dinner. Yeah, let's have a barbeque." Lotte giggled and went in search of some sticks.

Uwe sharpened them with his pocketknife and handed them back to her.

"What's the matter?" he asked.

"A slingshot, a pocketknife...what else do you have hidden in those pockets of yours?"

"Well, that's one good thing we learned with the *Hitlerjugend*. Always be prepared." He chuckled and watched her as she threaded the rabbit onto the sticks, and then rammed the sticks into the earth, leaving the animal hanging over the fire. Then they settled on the ground, side by side, watching their dinner roast, turning it every so often.

"I'm worried. I've never been on my own," Lotte said into the silence.

"Me too. And I feel guilty for leaving my mom alone. She must be out of her mind."

"Aunt Lydia will be crazy with sorrow as well. She must suspect something awful has happened, because I believe I saw her standing at the window when I was shoved into the police car." Lotte stood up to turn the rabbit. "I never wanted to endanger her or my cousins."

"What about your mother?" Uwe asked.

"Oh, goodness." She had completely forgotten about her family. It wouldn't take long before Aunt Lydia called Mutter and told her that Lotte was missing. She took a deep breath, swallowing the lump in her throat. "Mutter will be frantic."

"Tell me about your family," Uwe said as he stared into the fire.

A piece of her heart chipped off as she thought about them all. "You met my mother when she was here earlier this year, right?"

Uwe nodded.

"I'm the youngest. Baby, they like to call me." She made a face, and he chuckled in response. "Vater and Richard are missing somewhere in Russia. My two sisters live in Berlin. Anna is a nurse."

"I take it she hasn't joined up?"

"God, no. Anna never wanted to become a nurse in the first place. Ever since I can remember, she's been driven by ambition, has dreamed of becoming a biologist. But my parents opposed that. They said it was unheard of for a girl to be a scientist." Lotte thought of the many times Anna had battled with her parents. Anna's arguments that a woman had the right to choose her own destiny, and her mention of female scientists like Marie Curie or Lise Meitner, fell on deaf ears. After the outbreak of war, Anna had succumbed and given up her futile battle fighting both her conservative parents and the Nazis, who believed the place for a woman was her home and hearth.

"So, she became a nurse?" Uwe interrupted her thoughts.

"Yes. It seemed the logical thing to do. But my ambitious sister can't fool me. I'm pretty sure she'll bring up the topic of going to university again after the war.

"I can see a family pattern here. Two spitfire sisters. What about the third one?"

"Ursula. She's the oldest. She's totally different than Anna and me. You can't imagine how *good* my sister is. She's never once gotten into hot water. Not with our parents. Not at school. She has always followed the rules to a T. Ursula is obedient to a fault."

"You sure she's your sister?" Uwe teased.

"Well, some people do say she and Anna look like twins.

So yes, there's some family resemblance." Lotte laughed and watched as Uwe got up to turn the rabbit. He cut off a chunk with his pocket knife and handed it to her. "Here, try it."

The smell of the roasted meat reached her nostrils, and her mouth watered. Uwe's eyes clung to her mouth as she chewed on the rabbit, causing her head to swirl and momentarily forget where she was.

"A few more minutes," she said after swallowing.

"Is she a nurse, too?"

"Who?" After noticing his eyes, Lotte had all but forgotten their conversation.

"Your sister, Ursula."

"Oh, no. She can't stand the sight of blood. She's a prison guard." Lotte took a deep breath, inhaling the scent of roasted rabbit.

His eyes widened. "Baloney."

"No, really, it's true. She hates her job, but when the labor service bureau assigned her to become a prison guard, she raised no objection. As I said, she always does what she's told."

"Weren't you at her wedding in January?" Uwe asked.

"You remember?" Lotte raised an eyebrow, and he cast his eyes downwards. "It was wacky. A marriage by proxy. Can you imagine? My sister actually married a steel helmet. Her fiancé couldn't even come home for his own wedding."

"Our food should be ready." Uwe expertly pulled the rabbit off the spit and divided it into two halves. He gave Lotte the same size portion as he took, but she wasn't having any of that.

"You're bigger than I am and doing more of the heavy work. You need to eat more."

Uwe argued, but in the end, he cut off a chunk from her portion. Then they ate the tasty animal with their fingers like barbarians and drank water from the bucket.

Being in the woods with Uwe was fun. It could have been carefree if it weren't for the reason why they were there.

"Hans and his father are out for revenge. Do you think they can find us here?" Lotte asked in a shallow voice.

"I don't know. We're safe here for now."

Lotte propped herself on her elbows and sighed. "I'm a fraud, I see that now."

"Why do you say that? You're anything but a fraud."

"Look at me. I've been in Kleindorf almost three years, milking those damn cows. When, for the first time ever, I get the chance to do something really important, I mess it up and get caught."

"You didn't mess up, these things happen."

"To me...yes. They wouldn't happen to Ursula, or Anna, or anyone else." She buried her head in her hands and continued in a grave voice, "I wish I'd listened to my mother and kept my mouth shut. See where being so impulsive got me?" Her voice dropped to a murmur: "Telling Hans he's a coward was a horrible mistake."

"You did that?" At the alarm in Uwe's voice, she looked up and stared into his blue eyes, full of concern.

"Yes. I believe my exact words were, 'You're nothing more than a Nazi coward hiding behind your father's coattails.'"

"No wonder he was livid," Uwe said and cocked his head

to the side. "Never tell a lad he's a coward. That's about the worst thing you can say."

"I guess I learned that the hard way." Lotte stood and gathered thc remains of their meal to bury them in the earth.

Later, they walked to the creek and washed up, brushing their teeth with their fingers. Then Uwe carried another bucket of fresh water back to the hut.

Life over the next days carried on in a similar fashion, with Uwe killing some small animal for their dinner and Lotte finding wild lettuce, mushrooms, and berries to supplement their meals. For two glorious days, they pretended they were camping out, and then their situation changed.

CHAPTER 15

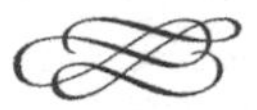

One day after lunch, they were lazing in front of the hut when voices wafted from the thick forest. Uwe raised his head in alarm and motioned for Lotte to crawl inside the hut. They huddled in the corner, scarcely hidden by the straw mattress, and waited. Lotte's mind conjured up sounds of footsteps and images of SS men bursting through the door.

After sitting almost an hour in complete silence, they dared venture outside again. They perked up their ears, but no sounds except for the wind could be heard.

"Whoever it was, he's gone," Uwe said and looked up into the sky where the sun was already hanging low.

"I was so scared," Lotte admitted as she watched the goosebumps on her arms disappear.

Uwe took a step towards her and wrapped his strong arms around her. The warmth of his body dispersed her fear and made the images of SS men in black uniforms fade away.

Instead, she became extremely aware of the pressure of his arms against her body and his masculine smell. Heat rose in her chest, sending her heart thumping faster. She tipped up her face. For a moment, their eyes locked, and then his lips were on hers in a tender touch.

Instinctively, she opened her lips and felt his tongue explore her mouth with an unrivaled urgency. The pressure of his arms intensified as he pulled her flush against him, oblivious to anything except their feelings for each other. Then he skimmed his hands down her back, and Lotte sighed in pleasure.

She gripped his shoulders, holding onto them like a drowning woman to a lifeline. This kiss, unlike their previous one, showed no signs of hesitancy or nerves. It was sweet first love between two people who had come face to face with their human frailty.

"That was close," Lotte murmured against his cheek as his lips skimmed over her jaw.

"Yes." He brought his lips back to hers once more, and after a lingering kiss, he hugged her close, burying his face in the crook of her shoulder. "God, I wish this war was over."

"Me too." She sat down on the grass, patting the space beside her. Uwe joined her, and she cuddled into his arm, letting the fear, worry, and tension seep out of her body.

"What did you want to be before the war?" she asked him quietly.

He didn't hesitate. "A forest warden, like my father. I love the stillness. The distinctive smell of the air. The twilight under the trees. The sounds of the animals. I even love the sweat running down my back when I'm chopping up trees."

Lotte giggled and ran her fingertips down his back. "Like this?"

"You slay me, but no, that's even better." Uwe kissed the tip of her nose. "How about you? What did you want to be before the war?"

"I have no idea. But I can tell you what I don't want. I refuse to blindly follow orders, to keep my mouth shut when I see injustice, to obey rules that don't make sense."

Uwe grinned, but the expression carried a hint of sadness. "I'll bet you were a troublesome youngster."

"Possibly. My favorite time of the year was summer break."

"No teachers telling you what to do?" he surmised.

"Exactly. My brother, sisters, and I would take a trip to the lake with my parents. Richard and I would spend the day swimming, running around, climbing trees...while my sisters gushed about boys I thought were truly awful." Lotte sighed at the memory of happier times before the war. Ursula and Anna had been eighteen and seventeen, and it seemed all they talked about was boys.

Uwe chuckled. "Most boys in their younger years are truly awful where girls are concerned, so you weren't far off."

Some stay awful when they grow up. "I miss those days."

"Me, too. And I will miss this place." Uwe ruffled her hair and smiled, but she could see the sadness in his eyes. "We can't stay here. Whoever was here will be back."

She nodded. "I wish I could talk to my sisters. They would know what to do."

"Would you actually listen to their advice?" Uwe teased her, trying to lighten the mood that had become oppressive.

"Sometimes. I was always so independent…"

"And now you're not?"

Lotte blushed. "I guess I still am. But I promise never to speak out of turn if I only get to see my family again."

"Would you still help Rachel if you knew things were going to turn out this way?"

"Yes! I don't regret helping Rachel and her siblings get someplace safe. The fact I regret is acting rashly and without thinking things through properly." A worrisome thought entered her mind. "I hope Irmhild is safe."

"Why wouldn't she be?" The confused look on Uwe's face reminded her that he didn't know.

She glanced at him. "She was the one who stole the forms from the town hall to make fake papers for the Epstein siblings."

"Geez. You and Irmhild faked papers?" The admiration on his face compensated her for many of the bad experiences she'd gone through.

"We did. They're now one hundred percent Aryan. Nobody will be searching for Karin Müller and her siblings." Lotte explained how they'd gone about producing new identities for their friends while Uwe listened in awe.

When she finished, he held her close. "I'm sure Irmhild is fine. The nuns in the convent won't examine the papers too closely."

"What about us? Where can we go?" The fear crept back upon Lotte as she pondered the difficulties they faced.

"What about Switzerland?" Uwe shrugged.

She whipped her head in his direction. "Switzerland? Isn't that too far to walk?"

Uwe was quiet for a moment. "From what I heard it's three hours by train. So maybe a hundred miles?" He looked at her dirty plimsolls and his sturdy boots. "Call it bonkers, but I believe we can make it. We could walk at night and hide during the day."

"Four or five days to reach safety." Lotte's heart was thumping against her ribs. "Do you know how to get there?"

"Not exactly, but if we follow the main road southwest until we reach Lake Constance, we should be fine."

She considered the suggestion for a long while, letting all the horrid szenarios play over in her mind. "We should leave tonight," Lotte said, moving away from him and sitting up. A growing thrill took possession of her. They would outwit the Nazis, and once they'd settled in Switzerland, she would write a letter to Mutter and her sisters with all the exciting details about this adventure.

"Yes. Let's return to the main road after nightfall and see how far we can get the first night." Uwe sounded more certain of himself the longer they talked, making plans for the time they reached neutral Switzerland.

"Can you imagine not having to live with Nazis controlling every second of our lives?" Lotte beamed at him, her expression one of wonder.

"I can. Once we cross the border, we'll make new lives for ourselves." Uwe jumped to his feet, then he reached down and pulled her up.

"Right now, I'm happier than I have been in months." Lotte walked into his arms and lifted her face for his kiss. She pushed up on her tiptoes to get closer to him, and he chuckled, clasping her around the waist and holding her up. When he kissed her, the world around her sank into oblivion. Uwe traced her lips with his tongue, and Lotte's stomach did a little flip.

"We can do this," he said after he broke the long kiss and looked down into her green eyes. "I know we can."

CHAPTER 16

They spent the next hour gathering provisions they could easily carry with them before lying down inside the hut. Uwe had decided to try and sleep a few hours in the afternoon before embarking on their journey at nightfall.

But the thrill of this new adventure kept Lotte wide awake, and judging by Uwe's breathing, he felt the same. She propped herself on her elbows to study his handsome face. His deep blue eyes were closed while the curved lips lay slightly opened in a smile, revealing a row of white teeth. After being away from civilization for several days, the beginning of a beard was sprouting on the soft skin of his cheeks.

She couldn't resist, and traced a finger along his jawline. He opened his eyes, and his breathing sped up. Lotte hesitated, not sure what to do next, but she needn't have worried because Uwe grabbed her tight, rolled them over, and kissed her with a passion she'd never experienced before.

Before things went too far, she broke the kiss and snuggled up into his embrace, letting his strength and confidence block out all thoughts of the looming evil. She dreamed of a bright future with Uwe in Switzerland.

"We should find something to eat before we leave," he interrupted her daydreams.

"Good idea," Lotte agreed even though she was reluctant to leave his warm embrace. But they had a long journey ahead of them.

They walked to the creek. The clear water gurgled like a happy giggle, causing tiny rapids as it flowed across the stones in the streambed. Lotte had just finished drinking and washing up when she heard it. The baying of dogs. She turned to look at Uwe to ask if he'd heard it too.

"Shit! We have to run!" He took off to her left, and she dashed after him. Branches and bushes scratched at her bare legs, but she didn't stop or cry out. Her heart thundered in her throat as she ran as fast as she could.

Uwe darted between the trees with an ease she found hard to follow. She did her best not to lose him, ignoring the scratches on her legs, the stitches in the side, and the shortage of oxygen, and kept running.

She knew when the men searching for them found the hut, as a loud cry went up and the sound of others crashing through the forest increased. *Don't stop. Keep running.* In front of her, Uwe darted to his right, his feet splashing as he crossed a shallow stream. Lotte followed him, her new shoes becoming soaked in the cold water, but she couldn't care less about her clothing or her looks. No doubt, the men hunting them were devoted followers of Herr Keller and the Party, and she had no doubt whatsoever about her fate should she be caught.

"Shit! Go back!" Uwe shouted a second later, grabbing her arm and spinning her around to dash back across the stream.

Lotte got a brief glimpse of men coming towards them, and then she heard the sound of the dogs being turned loose. *I can't outrun a bloody dog.*

They made it across the stream, but before they could go in a different direction, two SS men stepped from the thicket, their guns raised point-blank at them. The dogs splashed across the stream, and Lotte looked over her shoulder to see the vicious German Shepherds standing a mere three feet away from her, intent on tearing her and Uwe apart if they ran again. Lotte's blood froze in her veins, and even if she wanted to, she would have been unable to move. The SS men approached, and one of them grabbed the dogs' collars, holding them at bay while the other one barked commands at Lotte and Uwe.

"Hände hoch!"

She raised her hands and could see from the corner of her eye Uwe doing the same. The dogs leashed again, another SS officer appeared, glancing at the two frightened adolescents.

"He's the deserter." He nodded his chin in Uwe's direction. "Give him what he deserves."

The next seconds passed as if in slow motion, and Lotte's scream sent the birds in the trees scattering in all directions. Her glance darted from the SS officer pulling the trigger on his gun to Uwe's terrified face a split-second before the bullet hit him between the eyes.

"No!" Lotte screamed and launched herself towards Uwe but was captured mid-air by the third man while Uwe dropped to the ground, blood blooming across his forehead.

"A masterly shot," congratulated the SS man holding the dogs.

"Indeed," the first one answered. "It's good to get some practice on a live target."

"Killers! Bastards! Let me down!" she screamed, kicking, scratching and biting her captor.

"Why don't we shoot that one, too? Let her loose, and I'll see if I can take her down with a single bullet."

Lotte stopped kicking as the urge to vomit built inside her throat. After witnessing the cold-blooded murder, she almost yearned to share Uwe's fate.

"No. Sorry to disappoint you, but Chief Keller wants her alive."

Lotte wasn't sure whether that was a good or a bad thing, but either way, she didn't have a say. Her captor silenced her struggle with a well-targeted blow to her temple and then tossed a half-benumbed Lotte over his shoulder. He carried her for what seemed an eternity, until they reached a dirt road where a truck was waiting.

The SS man dumped her on the ground next to the truck. Her entire body aching from the bad treatment, she opened her eyes and thought she'd died and gone to hell. Hans was grinning down at her, pure evil in his eyes. She scrambled backward but came up against the tires of the vehicle.

"Hello, Lotte. I hoped we'd meet again." Hans reached

down and hauled her up, shoving her into the back of the vehicle before yelling something to one of the SS men who cuffed her hands behind her back.

"You bastard! They killed Uwe! He was your friend!"

"Uwe was a fool." Hans shoved her backward, causing her to fall onto her bound hands, leaving her unable to defend herself. Panic spread throughout every cell of her body as she observed how he licked his lips. "And you are, too. Why else would you choose him over me?"

Lotte tried to kick him as he reached his hands beneath the hem of her dress, but he caught her legs with his right hand and pressed them down while he shoved his left hand between her thighs, groping her crotch painfully.

Too petrified to look away, she began to cry for a different reason now, scared beyond comprehension at the look on Hans' face. The sound of her underwear ripping apart made her wince, but that was nothing compared to his fingers sliding higher between her legs and probing parts of her anatomy that no man had ever touched before. She couldn't control her sobbing and trembled at the prospect of what else he might do next.

"You're nothing but a whore. I bet Uwe enjoyed getting between these filthy thighs. Don't worry, I'll make sure you don't remember anything but me down there."

After several more humiliating and painful minutes, she heard the impatient voice of one of the SS men. "What are we waiting for? We don't have all day!"

"Coming," Hans called out and pinched her soft flesh in a painful grip before removing his hand. "Something for you to remember me by until I see you later." He jumped off the truck bed and several seconds later, the engine started.

Lotte curled into the corner, struggling not to be tossed around every time the truck hit a pothole. Her brain was clogged, and her body ached, but she kept her focus on one thing – revenge for Uwe's death.

One day those vile killers would get the punishment they deserved.

CHAPTER 17

The truck stopped, and the SS officers hauled her into a building she didn't recognize. Inside, they shoved her into an interrogation room.

"Let the Gestapo have their fun with her," one of them said as he handcuffed her to the chair.

Gestapo? All the blood drained from her face, and she would have fallen off the chair if it weren't for the cuffs. Moments later, the door opened, and two Gestapo officers entered. One of them was in his forties, while the other one wasn't much older than twenty.

"Heil Hitler." Heels clicked, and arms shot into the air.

"Thanks, we'll take over," the older Gestapo officer said and then nudged his colleague forward, mumbling something along the lines that he had more important cases to solve.

The younger officer took a chair, placed it in front of her and sat astride it until his steel-blue eyes were level with hers. Lotte could barely breathe and expected the worst. The Gestapo wasn't exactly known for using kid gloves. But much to her surprise, the young man asked, "Would you like some water?"

She could only nod.

His colleague brought a cup of water and held it to her lips as she drank. Once she finished, he stepped away and the young officer with the intense eyes asked, "Tell us about the Jews."

Lotte swallowed hard. "The Jews?"

"Rachel and Mindel Epstein. They came to you for help?"

She nodded to gain a few moments to think while her brain worked in overdrive. They didn't know about the boys? Was it possible Hans' father hadn't told them the exact number of children she had been hiding? Had he even told the Gestapo that they'd escaped from his prison?

"They were neighbors, and one day, Rachel and her baby sister showed up at the barn while I was milking the cows."

"What did they want?"

"A place to stay. Their parents had been arrested."

"So you hid them?"

Lotte nodded. "The little one was only four years old."

The young officer stared into her eyes, seeming to see into her soul. "Whom did you tell?"

"Nobody. I…my aunt would never have approved." It was only half a lie. "I felt empathy for the little girl, she looked so cute."

The young officer sighed. "They were Jews. They are a blight upon Germany, undermining the Führer's quest to create a pure master race. We can't have sympathy even for the cutest-looking child. It's a crime against a bright and strong future of our Fatherland."

She licked her dry lips, trying to look repentant.

"Even the Jews who appear to be the best citizens are in disguise. They are only here to bring doom to our country. They have already started the war, and even a single Jew who remains within our borders could bring the entire nation down."

Lotte listened, everything within her revolting at what he said. Rachel and her family had never caused anyone to suffer. She wanted to argue with the Gestapo officer, tell him how stupid this was, but she bit her tongue. The image of Uwe falling to the ground entered her mind. The tiny hole in his forehead. A drop of red. Her sharp tongue had caused his death.

"I'm so sorry," she murmured, tears filling her eyes.

The officer's expression softened, taking her by surprise. *He thinks I'm sorry for helping Rachel.*

"I'm sorry I ever helped them, I had no idea. The last thing I want is to cause harm to our country."

"War is tough and requires us all to make hard decisions. The greater scheme of things is not easy to understand, especially if you're just a female."

Her entire being rebelled, but she managed to cast down her glance and nod. Remembering Irmhild's advice to sweet talk Hans, she smiled at the young man. "You're right. I'm only a schoolgirl, and I had no idea my actions could have such an impact on the Fatherland." She batted her eyelashes at him. That had an instant effect, and he actually smiled, clearly smitten with her good looks.

After some more questions back and forth, he glanced at the older officer, who nodded and pointed his chin at the door. Apparently, they had more important things to do than question her. The young man stood and undid her cuffs. "I'll let you go this time with only a warning."

"Thank you so much, officer. I promise to be a good German and not be swayed by any more Jews." Lotte's heart bloomed with relief. From his expression, it was obvious she was saying all the right things, and she was very proud of herself.

"You'll have to sign your confession in the anteroom," he said and followed his colleague out the door in a hurry.

Lotte lingered for a moment, not sure what was expected of her, but then she heard angry voices from the anteroom and approached the door to have a peek. Her luck was running out.

"I'm telling you, this girl is nothing but trouble," Herr Keller said in a loud voice and then continued to list all her heinous deeds, including coaxing Uwe to desert and attempting to seduce Hans into helping her hide the Jews. With every word that Herr Keller uttered, she blanched some more and staggered with rage.

Once the mayor ended his speech, the young Gestapo officer turned to cast her a disgusted glance. "It seems this is not the first time you've been in trouble. Mayor Keller insists you be sent to social reintegration."

Her mouth fell open. "But you said–"

"Again, I've been informed of your previous behavior. My decision is final. You'll be sent to the women's work camp in Ravensbrück. Heil Hitler!" The Gestapo officer saluted.

"Heil Hitler," Lotte murmured, near to tears. Then they left her alone in the interrogation room.

CHAPTER 18

Lotte shuddered despite the warmth of the late summer day.

She'd been to Ravensbrück with her parents before the war. It was located about sixty miles north of her hometown of Berlin – a lovely place in the huge Uckermärkische lake district amidst vast greenery. It couldn't be that bad if she were sent to such a lovely place, right?

A work camp, the Gestapo officer had called it. Work, she could handle. At Aunt Lydia's farm, they sometimes worked for ten or twelve hours a day during harvest. No, work didn't scare her.

She just hoped her mother could visit every now and then. *Mutter. She'll be so disappointed.* Tears rolled down her cheeks. *I'll beg her to forgive me for not listening to her. Please, God let them punish only me and not my mom, my sisters, or Aunt Lydia. They haven't done anything. It's all my fault.*

The next morning, Lotte was dragged to the train station. Together with dozens of other women, she was herded onto the platform where they had to wait for the train to come along.

Her stomach rumbling with hunger and her throat raspy, she longed for some water, but she didn't dare ask the SS officers with their guns pointing at the women. After what seemed an eternity, someone brought a barrel of stinking liquid, but by then the women were so thirsty, they didn't care. Lotte gulped down a handful of the awful fluid, feeling only a momentary relief.

She hoped the train would arrive soon, and she'd be lucky enough to snatch a seat for the long journey to Ravensbrück. The last time she'd traveled with her mother to Berlin, it had taken them almost two days, including the several interruptions when everyone had to leave the train because of approaching enemy bombers.

When the train arrived, her jaw fell to the floor. It was one long row of cattle wagons, all of them filled to the tops with desperate women. *There's no way I'm boarding one of those wagons. People put on a cattle train never return to tell the tale.*

But when the SS officers made generous use of their batons, Lotte straightened her spine and followed the other women into the overcrowded wagon. She wrinkled her nose at the horrendous smell, a mixture of excrement, sweat, and fear that made her gag.

Lotte tried to find space next to the wall of the car, hoping for fresh air coming in through the slats, but she kept getting jostled out of the way. The air buzzed with sobs, desperate prayers, and angry imprecations, only some of them in German. The oppressive heat sent sweat running down Lotte's forehead, but she couldn't even raise her hand to wipe it away, such was the crush inside the train car.

After endless hours of standing back to back with the other prisoners, her cramping legs gave way, and she would have collapsed on the floor if she weren't pressed tight against several other women. With each turn the train took, a sea of bodies swayed from one side to the other. As the train suddenly stopped, Lotte was pressed against the wall, the weight of dozens of women squeezing the air out of her lungs. Still struggling for breath, she noticed the car door opening, a swift breeze of cool air reaching her nostrils.

But moments later, another rush of terrified women was shoved into the full cattle car. How? She had no idea. But even though there was no room left inside, the train stopped several more times to pick up more prisoners. Lotte must have succumbed to her exhaustion because when she opened her eyes again, it was dark outside and the temperature had dropped.

After traveling for the entire day, Lotte's tongue stuck against the roof of her mouth, but there was no respite. In the wee hours of the morning, the train finally arrived at its destination.

"Raus! Schnell!" Voices yelled to make everyone hurry out of the cattle car. Lotte stumbled to the ground, where the women were told to stand in a straight line before walking about half an hour to the camp.

At first, Lotte welcomed leaving the train. She even quirked her lips up in something similar to a smile as she noticed the female guards wearing a uniform similar to the one her sister wore as a prison officer. But the smile quickly dropped from her face when one of the guards lashed

Lotte's arm because she didn't march in line with the woman in front.

Her sister didn't have a whip, and Ursula prided herself that she'd never used her baton. But these women did. Frequently and with apparent joy. Every little offense was countered with a lash or a stroke. When a woman couldn't keep up and fell to the ground, Lotte's instinctive reaction to help earned her another lash.

"Keep going," the guard yelled.

More and more women lagged behind, and that's when Lotte heard it – barking dogs. And then the most awful sound of screeching women chilled her to the core.

This time, Lotte didn't miss a step. She walked on, eyes fixed on the back of the woman in front, blocking out anything and everything around her.

She didn't see the beautiful lake in the distance, nor the forest of pine and birch trees around the compound, didn't notice the lovely town they were marched through. She didn't even hear the sound of shutters being closed in the houses they walked past. But she couldn't help noticing the strange odor in the air, coming from a dark cloud of smoke rising in the distance.

A wave of homesickness swept over her. This was the closest she'd been to Berlin in many months, and yet it was so far away. As they reached the concrete wall dividing the campgrounds from the outside world, a bevy of male guards appeared out of nowhere and howled at the newcomers.

Even with all she had been through, Lotte had never been more scared in her life than in that moment. She almost jumped when she had to walk past another German Shepherd snapping his jaws and growling ferociously. In front of her, one woman lost control and ran away. To where, Lotte had no idea.

One of the guards gave a sickly laugh and released the dog. The animal jumped onto the terrified woman, biting and tearing at her flesh as she screamed in terror and pain. Lotte's stomach revolted at the morbid spectacle, but she somehow managed to hold herself upright. The guards clapped their hands, praising the dog, and pointing to where the now dead woman lay.

Lotte was pushed and prodded towards the entrance and the looming walls that concealed the prison. She thought she'd endured the worst, but nothing could have prepared her for the sight that awaited her upon walking through the gate.

Rows upon rows of long buildings with small windows and only one entrance and exit door apiece lay before her. Where there had been green grass and flowers growing outside the camp, here there was nothing beautiful. Lotte swallowed as fear like she'd never known tried to overwhelm her. She put one foot in front of the other, intent on not angering the guards that were yelling at the long line of women to keep them moving.

The guards separated the new arrivals into two groups. Old and weak women on one side, strong and healthy ones to the other. Lotte didn't mind joining the group of young women, she just hoped the old ones would be taken to a nicer place.

They started walking again, the women forced into a group rather than a line. Passing the white buildings that turned out to be the dormitories, Lotte noticed the inmates already there. Bald, skeletal figures wore identical blue-and-white striped dresses with white kerchiefs. They barely resembled human beings, looking instead like some horrible creatures escaped from a horror motion picture: walking skeletons of misery.

"Monsters," a woman cried out, "please keep those monsters away."

The reaction of the guards was an ugly laugh and the crack of a whip. Lotte instinctively ducked her head, the evidence of the fate awaiting her taking her breath away. Still, she continued to walk, one foot after the other, sticking to the center of the group because she'd quickly learned that was the best place to avoid being struck by the guards or nipped by the dogs.

"Lotte?" A harsh whisper called her name.

Lotte peered in the direction of the voice without moving her head and saw Irmhild meandering cautiously through the group of women towards her.

"Goodness, Irmhild, you too?" Lotte breathed, looking straight ahead, putting one foot in front of the other.

Her friend's eyes looked terrified. "They caught Rachel and Mindel with the fake papers on them. It was easy enough for the mayor to deduce that I had made them."

"I'm so sorry," Lotte whispered. "It's all my fault." How many more casualties would her rash actions cause?

"Herr Keller was livid because Aron and Israel had escaped. He even lied to the Gestapo about the number of children in hiding because he didn't want to be punished for his mistakes."

"At least that's something." She moved her hand to touch Irmhild's for a short moment, and a sliver of hope took hold of her. Guilt for dragging her friend into this weighed heavily on Lotte's soul, but at the same time, she took solace in the fact that she wasn't in this nightmare on her own.

The group of women had come to a halt in front of a building with the inscription *Brausebad* – shower room. Lotte sighed. Her summer dress stuck to her skin and she was covered in sweat and dirt from head to toe. A shower would be a welcome reprieve after this hellish train ride.

"Strip naked," the guards yelled at them.

Shame flushed her cheeks as she looked at Irmhild, who had the same expression of debasement on her face. To make things worse, a large group of SS men had followed the women to the showers, leaning onto their guns while leering and cheering at the group of terrified women.

"You need an extra invitation?" a female guard hissed, cracking her horrid whip. It ripped right through Lotte's summer dress, leaving a burning mark on her back. Gritting her teeth at the agonizing pain, she unbuttoned her dress and pulled it over her head.

When she was down to nothing but her underpants, which were already ripped from Hans' rough treatment of her, she hesitated. No man had ever seen her naked before, let alone a lewd group of them. Memories of Hans' assault rushed to her brain. How much worse could this get?

"Get those ratty things off and throw them over here," a female guard screamed in her face, slapping her legs with the baton in her hand.

"That's right, you floozy. Get those clothes off and show us those tits and ass." The SS men jeered and hooted, making crude comments, some of which Lotte didn't even understand.

Lotte flinched, but removed her underwear and then

tossed the ripped garment onto the pile in front of her. The guard lifted it up with her baton and showed it to the cheering men. "Looks like this one had a little fun before her arrest."

"Come here, and we can all have some fun," another uniformed man hooted with delight.

Lotte turned crimson at the implication and had to bite her tongue to hold back her protest. It was the most debasing and terrifying situation she'd ever experienced in her life. In fact, since she'd been caught in the forest with Uwe, her life had been a succession of steadily deteriorating experiences.

Will this ever end?

Thankfully, she was ordered to pick up her shoes and enter the shower building – away from the leering SS men. But inside, the next horror awaited her. Separated into two groups, the women of the first group were forced into the barber chair. *Clip, clip* went the shears, stripping the women of their femininity, leaving them with bald skulls devoid of eyebrows, and no trace of hair between their legs.

Lotte closed her eyes, but she couldn't block out the sobs of formerly beautiful women reduced to frumps. She curled a strand of her hair around her finger. While she'd always disliked the way her curls couldn't be tamed, she most definitely didn't want to lose them.

When it was her turn to mount the barber's chair, she was relieved when the man was done using the shears on her, but the reprieve lasted only for a split-second. Moments later, her feet were strapped in stirrups, and he held up a duck beak–shaped metallic instrument. Without any warning, he shoved it inside her, violently pushing the two sides apart, without consideration for her tender flesh.

Lotte could no longer contain her tears and sobbed as his rubber-clad finger followed the instrument inside, where he poked and probed and tormented. She didn't notice when he retrieved his finger, forced her mouth open and jolted her teeth with the same finger that had just been inside her down there. A nurse standing nearby dutifully jotted down his comments on a clipboard.

Despite the explanation of testing the newcomers for venereal disease, Lotte didn't have to be the sister of a nurse to know this wasn't true. Since neither the instrument nor his rubber gloves were cleaned or changed between patients, this procedure was clearly intended to humiliate and debase.

Like a zombie, she climbed from the chair and shuffled into the next room to take an icy shower. At least she managed to quench part of her thirst by catching the water with her mouth. Jittering, she picked up her shoes and carried them to the assembly space where the roll call took place. After standing naked in line for hours, she was given an ugly blue-and-white striped dress made of rough drill with a white kerchief to wear.

Despite the scratchy material, it was a respite to be dressed again.

Lotte dared a glance at Irmhild and inched closer to her friend. Both of them received a green triangle of cloth and their prisoner number to be worn on her clothing at all times. She didn't need to ask what the consequences would be for disobeying. The green patch indicated they were common criminals. Whether that was a good thing or not, Lotte had no idea.

When they were ordered to march to the barracks, Lotte reached for Irmhild's hand, seeking a bit of comfort in this hostile world.

CHAPTER 19

Lotte's only solace was that she and Irmhild were assigned to the same barracks. The *Aufseherin,* as the guards were called, yelled into the barracks and an emaciated woman with a dead look in her eyes hurried to the entrance.

"Get these prisoners accommodated and have them attend roll call in ten minutes," the *Aufseherin* shouted.

"Yes, ma'am," the bald woman answered and motioned for Lotte and Irmhild to follow her.

Upon entering the dim building, Lotte held her nose at the disgusting stench of human excrement, sickness, and death. Bile rose in her throat, but she only imagined the punishment should she vomit all over herself, so she swallowed it down.

Bunk beds, three tiers high and barely five feet in length, lined the walls of the six large rooms inside the barracks. All of the rooms connected via a narrow hallway. The bald woman introduced herself as Verena and led them to a bunk bed.

“Welcome to hell on earth. Your bed is up there.” She pointed to the top bed. “We always put the newcomers on the top because they’re still strong enough to climb up.” Then she shuffled to another bunk, grabbed a blanket, and handed it to Irmhild. “You’re lucky, the owner died last night. You can have her blanket. Take good care of it. It will be your most precious belonging when winter sets in.”

Irmhild made to climb the bunk without the assistance of a ladder while Lotte waited for the woman to assign her a bed too.

Verena gave a dry cough. “When you’re ready, I’ll show you the facilities.”

“And me?” Lotte asked.

“You?”

“Where do I sleep?”

She pointed a finger. “Up there, with your friend.”

Lotte swallowed hard and sank onto the bottom bunk. The bare straw mattress filled with wood shavings scratched her legs. *I guess we won’t get a bed sheet either. At least I’ll share with Irmhild and not some stranger.*

Irmhild climbed down again, her eyes full of fear and disgust. Lotte grabbed her hand and whispered, “As long as we’re together, it’s not half as bad.”

Verena led them to the stinky latrine at the end of the barracks, a room with nothing but a dozen toilet bowls.

“You can use them during the assigned times, but never at night because the doors are shut. There will be pails by the entrance to each room in case of an emergency. Now hurry, or you'll be late for the roll call, and if that happens, everyone gets into trouble."

Lotte's stomach growled viciously.

"You never get used to the hunger," Verena murmured.

After having been forced to parade naked past the lewd SS men only hours ago, goosebumps rose on her skin as Lotte marched back the same way. She grazed her fingers across the scratchy material of her prisoner's uniform to make sure it was still there, protecting her against the awful glances violating her modesty.

Thousands and thousands of women poured onto the assembly place, each looking more ghostly and emaciated than the next one. The realization that she would soon look like the rest hit her like a hammer. A picture of human misery. *Dear God, what have I done?* Suddenly the idea of letting Hans kiss her didn't seem so bad anymore.

Every woman seemed to have an exact place to stand, except for the newcomers. Within her few hours in the camp, Lotte had already learned to never hesitate even for a split-second before carrying out an order from the guards. When the newcomers were yelled at to gather in the front rows, she sprinted forward to take her assigned place.

The roll call lasted for an eternity, and Lotte fought with fatigue, hunger, and cramping legs, but she neither staggered nor moved. Not until a man who was introduced as the doctor in charge ordered all the newcomers to undress.

The sun had long set behind the trees looming over the prison wall reminiscent of an outside world, and the temperature had fallen considerably. Lotte neatly folded her prisoner dress and laid it at her feet the way she'd been told. Once she was finished, she stood erect, looking into the distance, beyond the prison walls. All the way back to Aunt Lydia's farm and her cozy, warm bed with the down blanket and the soft pillow.

The doctor, a nurse in tow, walked down the long line of women, stopping every few feet to utter a few words. When he reached Lotte, he glanced at her for a moment, and the nurse read from her list. "German. Seventeen. Social reintegration."

"Ammunition factory," the doctor said.

Despite the debasing situation, Lotte managed to hold her head high. She didn't even flinch when the woman next to her fell to the ground, and a guard rushed over, beating her with a baton until she crawled into place again.

"*Untauglich.* Block 7," the doctor said, and the nurse dutifully jotted it down.

Unfit? What does that mean? Lotte thought.

After hours of debilitating roll call, they were ordered to dress again and report in the morning to their line of work. Just as Lotte was sure her knees would buckle, it was finally time for dinner.

She hadn't expected whole milk, cheese, and bacon that were the norm at Aunt Lydia's, but what she received was far worse than she could ever have imagined. Fifty grams of bread and a watery soup with half a potato for each woman. The only abundant thing was smelly water to drink. Nothing that came close to soothing the hunger gnawing at her gut.

Back in their barracks, she learned that Irmhild had been assigned the same work.

"Ammunition factory? Lucky you," Verena said. "They treat the prisoners comparatively well. And as long as you're fit to work you have a chance to survive the daily selections."

Unfit, the doctor had said. *Block 7.* "What does Block 7 mean?" Lotte blurted out.

"It's the barracks for those who are too weak or sick to work. Once there, you never return," Verena answered with a hard voice.

"How long have you been here?" Lotte whispered.

A painful expression crossed Verena's face. "Years. I've been in other camps before, but this one is by far the worst."

With the woman's words ringing in her head, Lotte climbed up to her bunk. There, she held Irmhild tight before both of them fell into a coma-like sleep.

CHAPTER 20

The weeks passed and winter arrived, accompanied by snow and constant winds. Lotte was still wearing the prisoner's dress that barely shielded her against the punishing easterly winds. At least she still had the plimsolls her sisters had given her for her birthday. They had been a genuine blessing during her time at the labor camp, especially during the endless roll calls every morning and evening. Lotte pitied the women who wore sandals or went barefoot, with rags wrapped around their feet as their only protection.

Once again, she stood by Irmhild's side, doing her best not to stagger or faint. For hours and hours, they stood still, icy gusts tearing at their dresses. She had stopped looking when yet another woman – usually one of the older or weaker ones – fell to the ground. It never took more than a few seconds until an *Aufseherin* arrived, cracking her whip at the unfortunate soul.

The buzzing sound, though, followed by a bang and a

slap and a muttered scream managed to send her off-kilter every time. Any woman too emaciated and sick to get up again was left lying on the ground in the bitter cold. Her frozen corpse would later be hauled away.

Roll call was the most dreaded time of the day because here they were exposed to the moods of the guards, and the vagaries of the weather. At least during work in the ammunition factory – gruesome and exhausting as it was – they spent the time inside the heated factory, protected from wind and ice. Sometimes, the free workers would furtively hand them a morsel of bread or cheese.

Lotte knew that as German citizens, she and Irmhild had been given preferential treatment. Others had to work outside, digging ditches in the fields or carrying bricks.

Every day, new women arrived in this nightmarish hellhole, but it seemed like the same number of prisoners perished in this cesspool of sickness and starvation. The vicious doctor attended the roll call for selection every other day. This could mean one of two things: either selection for horrific medical experiments or for the gas chamber. At night, Lotte could see the high red flame shooting out of the crematorium chimney, and the stench of burned bodies permeated every inch of the camp.

But the alternative was worse. The ambitious Doctor Tretter was in his late thirties. Working on a groundbreaking advance in treating gas gangrene victims – both to please Hitler and for his treatise to become a professor of medicine at the University of Berlin – he regularly needed new human guinea pigs for his abhorrent experiments.

He usually chose Poles. Those women had been given the nickname *Króliki,* rabbits, and the entire camp pitied them for what they had to endure. Their screams reverberated throughout the camp, shaking not only the flimsy walls of the barracks but also setting the teeth of everyone who heard them on edge.

Many times, Lotte had tried to block out the screeching sound by putting her hands over her ears – to no avail. After hours of screaming, the women would be returned to their barracks and left to suffer. No treatment whatsoever was given to them.

Lotte scratched the wall behind her bunk with a stone. One hundred and five scratches. One hundred and five days since she and Irmhild had arrived.

Irmhild shivered next to her, and Lotte put her own blanket atop her friend. Irmhild had the chills and was burning up at the same time. Her sickness had started a few days earlier, but she had still managed to work through her shift at the factory. On the way back to the camp tonight, though, Lotte had been forced to half carry her friend.

"Typhus," Verena said after a short glance. "I'm afraid she won't make it through the night."

No. No. Irmhild can't die!

Irmhild weakly opened her eyes. "I'm sorry."

Lotte smoothed what little hair hadn't fallen out back from her forehead. "Whatever for?"

"For leaving you. It's my time. I can't do this any longer."

"No, don't say this. We've gone through so much – you'll be fine." Lotte swallowed back her tears, trying to instill hope.

"I…" Irmhild stopped mid-sentence and coughed.

Lotte wiped her forehead with a wet rag and then started to talk to her friend about better times. When they lived in Kleindorf and complained about the teachers at school. How Irmhild had been smitten with a boy. Their summer days. Eating ice cream at the river.

When she couldn't think of anything else to say, she looked down at her sick friend, gasping when Irmhild took her last ragged breaths.

I promise, one day I will avenge your death. I will make them pay. For you. For Uwe. For Rachel and Mindel.

Lotte didn't weep.

The women believed that anyone who wept at night would die the very next day. It was true. She'd witnessed it many a time. The moment a woman couldn't hold back her tears anymore, her will to live was broken.

She hugged Irmhild one last time before speaking aloud, "She's dead."

Two women offered to take on the task of removing Irmhild's body from the top bunk in exchange for her blanket. When Lotte only nodded, they grabbed her friend under the arms and dragged her towards the door of the barracks. Since it was already after curfew, she would have to lie there until morning, when the corpses were collected and either incinerated or tossed into a mass grave.

Alone now, Lotte wondered how much longer she would survive. She'd arrived at the camp, a healthy young woman on the cusp of womanhood, with shiny red hair and bright green eyes full of life.

And now? She wasn't much more than a walking skeleton, her skin hanging from her bones like the dress hung on her frame. Her formerly beautiful hair had taken on a grayish-red color and was falling out due to the stress, exhaustion, and poor food rations.

The last time she'd taken a shower was on the day of her arrival, and a constant itching reminded her of the lice and scabies infesting her skin and hair.

This night she didn't sleep, despite her constant exhaustion. Her mind was filled with memories of those who had already died. She saw Uwe's smiling face and felt his tender lips on hers. She saw Irmhild laughing with delight as they celebrated having faked the identification papers. She saw Rachel, joyous upon receiving the news that the convent would accept them. All of them gone, save for herself.

How much longer can I survive? Now that I'm alone.

CHAPTER 21

The next morning, Lotte had to endure roll call without Irmhild by her side. The missing comfort of a friendly soul constricted her chest, and she was cold – inside and out. It felt as if the very flame of her own spirit had been doused with Irmhild's death.

White snowflakes danced to the ground, covering the camp with a soft blanket. A kindergarten song came to her mind, calling on a white snowflake to make the long way from the clouds down to earth and settle on the window, painting flowers and leaves on the glass.

Schneeflöckchen, Weißröckchen,
wann kommst du geschneit?
Du wohnst in den Wolken,
dein Weg ist so weit.

. . .

Komm setz dich ans Fenster,
du lieblicher Stern,
malst Blumen und Blätter,
wir haben dich gern.

But today, Lotte didn't welcome the white flakes as she had as a child. Today, it meant her dress and shoes would be wet and icy most of the day. One flake settled on her nose, but she didn't dare to move and rub it away. It sat there, slowly melting, the icy drop sliding down her face until she caught it with her tongue.

As children, Lotte and her siblings had anxiously awaited the first snow of the year. They would rush out to play, launching snowballs at each other and building a snowman. After hours of play, they'd return home exhausted to the warm kitchen and their mother's hot chocolate and Christmas cookies.

How she missed her sisters. She hadn't seen Ursula and Anna in almost a year. *They may not even know where I am.* She truly was left alone in this hostile place.

Lotte shivered. Her arms no longer had feeling in them they were so cold, but still, the roll call went on – and on. They should be on their way to work already. Lotte almost crumpled with despair. If they arrived late, that would mean no lunch and working extra time in the evening.

She despised the gruesome work in the factory. Each day, she was left with red and burning eyes after peering through a magnifying glass, brazing and soldering minuscule parts, making weapons to help the Nazis kill people.

But on days like today, anything was better than

standing still in the assembly yard. At least the factory had a roof and was warm. In summer, it probably became a smoldering hell, if she lived long enough to find out.

Her mind still lingered on work when she heard stomping footsteps and focused on the approaching people.

God, no! Not the doctor, please! Now the roll call would take another hour or so. The vile doctor walked down the line in his shiny boots, thick woolen coat, fur hat, and black leather gloves. She'd give everything to possess only one of his warm garments.

The doctor stopped every so often to select a woman who seemed too sick to work. All of them would later be brought to the *Erschießungsgang,* the execution corridor. Once they were shot, the doctor declared them dead and signed the death certificate. Even in the concentration camp everything was written down and preserved on endless lists. Then the dentist went to work to gouge out any gold teeth.

Lotte clenched her jaw at the thought. *Bloody bastards, at least you won't find gold in my mouth.* But even without gold teeth, the Nazis would profit from her corpse. Bones were made into soap, hair woven to wool, and the ashes were used as fertilizer for the fields.

The doctor and a nurse approached Lotte's line. The nurse was wearing the usual uniform of the camp nurses, topped with a heavy woolen coat, fur hat, and leather gloves similar to the doctor's. Lotte couldn't see her face, but her posture had something familiar about it.

As the two of them approached, Lotte looked straight ahead, rose to her full height, and bit her lip and the inside of her cheek to make the blood rush to her face. It was a trick she'd learned from Verena to escape selection. A pale face could mean your death. Another thing Verena had impressed upon her was to never make eye contact. Ever.

The doctor came to a stop in front of her, and she knew he was looking her up and down, searching for signs of weakness. Lotte summoned the scraps of inner strength she still possessed and defied every adversity – the icy gusts, the snow, her fatigue, and her fear. She stood like a statue, her eyes boring into the doctor's chest until he moved to the next woman in line and said something.

"Yes, Doctor," the nurse said, and Lotte's head snapped up.

Anna!

Lotte stared straight into her sister's beautiful blue eyes. Long months of being subjected to cruel punishments for the tiniest offenses kept her mouth shut and her limbs still, despite the urge to scream and wrap her hands around her sister's neck.

No, strangling is too kind.

Anna's face showed no trace of recognition. She looked at Lotte as if she were just another prisoner. Another unfortunate soul, dehumanized, exploited, and tortured in every possible way.

I'm such a miserable being, my own sister doesn't recognize me. For a second, a tear started to form in her eye, but Lotte stubbornly willed it to go away. She'd endured worse. She wouldn't cry over her traitorous sister and risk dying the next day.

Out of the corner of her eye, she noticed Anna saying something to the doctor, and he nodded.

Anna turned on her heel and said aloud, "Doctor Tretter needs a volunteer for his medical experiments."

Lotte shivered once and then steeled herself from giving into the bitter cold. *How could Anna stoop so low as to help the Nazis with this most abominable work?*

Nobody moved, and the yard became silent enough to hear the snow fall. Tap. Tap. Tap. Lotte recoiled in fear, her ability to stand hanging on a thin thread. A woman behind her fell, and moments later, Lotte heard the whip cracking in the air. Then a scream. Then nothing.

Meanwhile, Anna had taken two more steps and stood directly in front of her, staring into her eyes. "You. Number 589452. Don't you want to volunteer? For a chance to live?"

Lotte nodded automatically, the oxygen leaving her lungs. Her own sister had just condemned her to a fate worse than eternal purgatory. "Yes."

Everyone around her seemed to deflate in relief that they hadn't been chosen.

"Follow me," Anna commanded and walked away.

Lotte obeyed, following her sister to the medical barracks and awaiting the worst.

CHAPTER 22

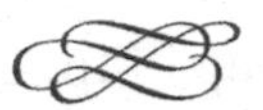

Lotte's chest was heaving with rage as she hurried after Anna, fists clenched and eyes cast down at her shoes...the very same plimsolls the traitorous woman in front of her had given her as a birthday gift. Suddenly, her feet itched as if they were covered in poison.

"An–" Lotte opened her mouth to blast her sister with all of the vitriol these last few months had created in her breast the moment Anna motioned for her to sit on the stretcher in the examination room. But her sister shook her head emphatically and placed a finger over her lips.

What the hell is she doing? Lotte pursed her lips, her eyes blazing anger that needed no words.

"No talking, Lotte," Anna whispered with a warning glare in her eyes that Lotte knew all too well. If Anna had *this* look, she meant it.

So, she did recognize me. But why is she here? And why did she choose me? Doesn't she know that every woman in this camp would rather be dead than a Króliki?

While Anna busied herself doing something on the other side of the room, Lotte sighed and bit back her questions. Moments later, Anna approached, a loaded syringe in her hand. Lotte's eyes widened with horror. In her former life outside the camp, she hadn't been afraid of syringes, unlike her sister Ursula, but now she cringed away. She wasn't sure she knew this Anna person anymore. Was she here to give her a merciful death by means of a lethal injection?

Anna grabbed her arm, swabbed it with alcohol and then injected the liquid into her muscle. A burning sensation spread through her arm.

"This is a typhus vaccine. Pretend to be sick. Do you understand?" Anna whispered.

What? Do I understand? No, I don't. You just condemned me to death.

Lotte looked at Anna with incomprehension. Typhus was what had taken Irmhild's life the night before, and once she started getting sick, she wouldn't be able to work. The Nazis had no use for those unable to work.

Lotte clenched her fists, her ragged nails making indentations in her palms as she struggled to keep quiet. Anna put the syringe away and then walked towards the door, meeting Lotte's eyes before opening it and mouthing, "Trust me."

Trust you?

Before Lotte could think of a response, Anna commanded, "Back to work, prisoner."

The *Aufseherin* was waiting outside to escort her to where the rest of her work colleagues were waiting. They were worried, but also understandably angry, because due to Lotte's delay they would now all have to go without lunch and work overtime. Not that lunch was something to look forward to.

Dear God, I hope Anna is here for a good reason.

Trust me. Those words echoed inside her head the rest of the day. She had a decision to make. Trust her sister. Or not.

It wasn't like she had a lot to lose either way.

At work, talking was strictly forbidden, but at night in the barracks, the other women assailed her with questions.

"What happened?"

"What did he do to you?"

"Does it hurt?"

"I don't know." Lotte wished she could answer them truthfully, but she wasn't even sure herself what exactly happened.

"What do you mean, you don't know? Did they knock you out?"

Lotte shook her head. "No. They injected me with something."

"What?"

"They didn't say. It stung." *It's a typhus vaccine. Pretend to be sick*. Anna's words came back to her. She looked at the women, allowing a very real fear to surface. "I don't know what it was, but it makes me feel weak. Burning up from the inside."

That much was true.

CHAPTER 23

Dinner that night was a somber affair, more so than usual. Seeing zombie-like creatures dragging themselves to the kitchen for food was a thing of normalcy, but today many of the women had feverishly glittering eyes and unusually bright red cheeks.

Lotte grabbed her ration of one slice of bread and a bowl full of potato soup. She gulped down the lukewarm soup, afraid the *Aufseherin* would take it away if she dallied, and felt like a lucky winner when she found a thumb-sized piece of potato at the bottom.

After this meal that wasn't even enough to mollify the gnawing pain in her stomach, Lotte trudged with everyone else to the assembly yard for the nightly roll call. At this time of the day, she didn't care anymore. The bitter cold had left her body without sensation, and her only worry was that she'd drop to the ground should she fall asleep.

She knew if she plopped down, she'd never stand up again, despite the beating, shouting, and kicking by the guards. As the guards continued down the line, shouting out number after number and waiting for the answer, an unexpected halt was called to the inspection, and the doctor appeared.

Again? Hasn't he caused enough suffering for one day?

"All prisoners report to the medical barracks," one of the guards yelled. "Single file. No talking."

Cries of alarm filled the air but were quickly quieted by the guards. Lotte cringed even as Anna's words once again flowed through her brain. *Trust me.* Did this have anything to do with the typhus vaccine she'd given her?

After hours of standing in line and having blood samples taken, the women were finally allowed into their barracks and fell into an exhausted sleep.

The next morning during roll call, Lotte's number was called, along with many, many others. They were separated from the rest of the prisoners and herded into the overflowing quarantine barracks. Block 7. The block from where nobody ever returned.

Lotte had thought her barracks was bad, but this one couldn't be real. The stench of disease and death stung in her nose. Most of the sick women had diarrhea and were already too weak to get up from the bunks they shared with five other women.

Rumor was that everyone infected with the dreaded disease would be left to die. The chances of recovering in these conditions were zero.

God, Anna, I do hope you have a plan.

It couldn't be her sister's scheme to let her perish in the quarantine barracks. Or could it? Her tired mind circled endlessly about Anna, the camp, the typhus epidemic, and her imminent death. But in one last effort, she climbed one of the top tier bunks and decided to trust her sister with her life and her future. If Anna thought this was a good idea, then Lotte wouldn't argue with her.

Soon, Lotte fell into an exhausted sleep, haunted by nightmares. Several times she woke and blinked against the bright light streaming through the shutters on the windows. *My goodness! I'll be late for work!* She was scrambling over bodies – asleep or dead – and down towards the exit of the barracks before remembering that she didn't have to work today.

Throughout the day, more and more women succumbed to the disease, and the air became thick with the putrid stench of rotting flesh. Lotte choked, but her stomach had been empty for so long, not even the bile rose.

Undertaker prisoners were sent inside with the task of clearing out the corpses and dumping them into the mass grave outside the barbed wire. They worked at their vile job way into the night. Usually, the corpses were cremated, but the Nazis were fearful that the disease would spread through the ashes used as fertilizer on the fields, and buried those who died of typhus outside the prison wall.

Several kitchen aids brought buckets of water. Dinner-time. Lotte climbed down to drink the smelly liquid and then sat on the floor to wait for food. But nothing happened. At long last, she heard tired and forced footsteps. *The kitchen aids. Finally.*

"Why should we waste this precious food on them? They'll all be dead by tomorrow anyway," a voice said.

"You're right," another voice answered, "let's bring that food to our barracks. We need it more."

Lotte gave a howling sound, but it went unnoticed amid the groaning and moaning of the sick women. She leaned against the wall and must have dozed off, because she woke to a shrill sound, the evening roll call alarm.

Out of habit, Lotte stumbled to her feet and hurried to take her assigned place in the assembly yard. But she found the entrance door to the barrack locked.

"Let me out, or I'll be late," she screamed, jolting the door until a hoarse voice reached her ears. "No more roll call for us. Not in this life."

Lotte's head snapped around to look into the bloodshot eyes of a bald woman with greenish-yellow skin. "What do you mean?"

"It's over. We're as good as dead."

Lotte struggled to return to her bunk and closed her eyes, wondering if Anna's plan had been such a good idea. It was only a matter of time before they found out she wasn't really sick, and then both she and Anna would be in dire straits.

CHAPTER 24

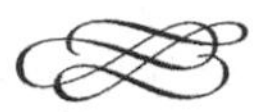

Lotte was shivering in the cold when the wake-up alarm echoed across the camp at four a.m. She started up, but then fell back on her bunk when she remembered that she didn't have to attend roll call or work. She hoped there would at least be food.

About half an hour later, the doors opened, signaling the arrival of someone with their morning rations. Lotte climbed from the bunk and got in line with the other women, weak from sickness, hunger, and cold.

When it was her turn in line, she glanced at the kitchen aid distributing the meager rations and saw a few steps behind her a guard and a nurse standing. *Anna.* A sudden rush of excitement coursed through Lotte's veins, but she didn't dare look at her sister, who dutifully jotted down on a clipboard which prisoners had made it through the night.

She didn't have much to write.

Lotte took her bowl of soup and retreated to gulp it down. It tasted even more rancid than usual. She cupped her hands around the tin, trying to draw some warmth into her stiff, frozen fingers, but there was little to draw from.

"You. Come here," the *Aufseherin* barked, pointing at Lotte and sending the other women scurrying backward. Lotte stood up and approached the guard, not sure what was expected of her.

Anna examined her briefly and then ordered the *Aufseherin*, "Bring this one to the doctor's office." Anna turned on her heel and walked away, leaving the guard to manhandle Lotte across the compound and into the medical barracks.

The guard knocked her baton into Lotte's back, and she fell across the threshold into the examination room.

"Thank you, that will be all for now," Anna told the guard and closed the door.

Lotte scrambled to her feet and stood in the middle of the room waiting. When Anna turned to face her, she whispered with a sad smile on her face, "Lotte, baby. I promise to get you out of here."

"How? How are you here?"

"To come and save you. Isn't that what sisters are for?"

Lotte couldn't believe her ears. Was she already delirious and imagined this conversation? "But how did you come to work here? Anna…the horrible things that happen here."

Anna pressed her lips together and nodded. "I befriended a nurse at my old hospital. Elisabeth previously worked here but had asked for a transfer because she couldn't stand the cruelties any longer. Since they were still looking for her replacement and with her recommendation, I got her old job. Ursula and I came up with a plan to get you out of here. The typhus epidemic was the opportunity I've been waiting for. This disease terrifies the Nazis because it spreads so quickly and there's no known remedy. The sick are quarantined rather than exterminated out of fear of contagion."

"I don't understand," Lotte mumbled. Her brain was so malnourished it couldn't follow the meaning of her sister's words.

"Since you're already in quarantine, the only thing I need is the doctor's signature on your death certificate. Then you'll be dumped outside the wall with the other corpses."

"In the mass grave?" Lotte blanched at the idea.

Anna put a hand on Lotte's arm, and Lotte felt her sister's strength jumping over into her body.

"You are crazy, you know?" Lotte tried to smile, but her face muscles refused the unusual expression.

"I'm sorry, sweetie, but the only way to leave this camp is with your feet first," Anna said.

The thought sent chills into her bones, and Lotte wondered whether she could pull it off without screaming in terror. But what alternative did she have? She took a deep breath and then nodded. "I'll do it. I don't want to die here."

"I don't want you to die here either. It will work. I promise." Anna smiled tenderly and hugged her.

With all the energy left inside her, Lotte hugged her sister back.

"I knew it," said a male voice.

CHAPTER 25

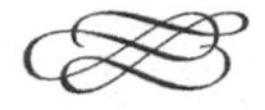

Anna and Lotte broke apart to see the doctor standing just inside the door, growling at them.

"Doctor Tretter, it's not what it looks like," Anna hurried to explain.

"Shut up. It's exactly what it looks like. You see, I'm not as dumb as you suppose me to be. The way you seemed to randomly select this prisoner was more than a little suspicious, and I did some research. She's your sister."

Anna blanched, and Lotte trembled.

He slammed the door behind him and walked towards them, rubbing his hands as if he was already enjoying whatever he was planning. Lotte had seen the evil glint in his eye many times before.

The perverted monster took a step toward Lotte, but not enough that he would actually be able to reach for her. After glancing at Lotte's dirty prisoner dress, emaciated figure, and limp hair, he sneered, "At one point in time, I'm sure all the boys were eager to sink into your body, but this place has a way of making most women undesirable. Worthless."

Anna gasped, but he shot her a look, and she pressed her lips together.

He walked around the table, making Anna back up to give him room, and continued his appraisal of Lotte. "You tested positive for typhus, so I'm sure you won't be with us much longer. Pity."

Leaning forward, he sniffed delicately and then reared back. "God, the stench of death is all over you. Filthy piece of trash, covered in lice."

Then he turned his attention to Anna. Lotte's eyes followed his gaze, and she saw not her sister, but a beautiful young woman, having just turned twenty-one on her last birthday, with shiny blonde hair, full lips, and a flawless complexion. She exhibited curves in all the places where Lotte had nothing but protruding bones covered with wrinkled skin.

"Now, you, on the other hand, *Schwester* Anna, I've had my eye on since you arrived. Young. Fresh. Meat on your bones a man can grab ahold of. And I'll bet you're a virgin to boot. Just what this doctor requires in payment for my silence." He stalked Anna across the room, and Lotte watched as her sister backed up and put up her hands to keep the doctor at bay. He removed his coat, tossing it onto the cabinet and then rolled up his sleeves.

Lotte gasped and intended to come to her sister's aid, but Anna shook her head. "Don't!"

"If you don't want me to summon the guards and have you both executed on the spot, you'll listen to your sister." The doctor gave a dirty laugh.

"Doctor Tretter, please, let my sister go," Anna begged.

His eyes swept down her body, lingering on her breasts. "I might…I might…but there will be a price to pay."

"Anything you want," Anna answered through thinned lips.

"I see we understand each other." He licked his lips. "I'll see to it that you will have some fun, too."

"Anna, please don't do this. Not for me," Lotte begged her.

"I have to. I promised Mutter," Anna answered with tears in her eyes. "Trust me."

Those words again! A horrible feeling washed over Lotte, and she wished she could do something. Anything. But she was powerless.

"If I let you do this…" Anna's voice broke off as the awful man reached out and slid his hand down the front of her body.

"Oh, you're going to let me do this. Make no mistake."

Lotte could see the effort it cost her sister to stand still and not cry. She couldn't take the spectacle any longer and closed her eyes.

"If I don't fight you, will you sign my sister's death certificate and let her go?" Anna bartered with the perverted man.

"Why do I care if I sign it now or tomorrow? She has typhus and will die anyway." Lotte cracked open her eyes just in time to see the man unbuttoning his pants. "But since you seem so attached to that piece of trash, I'll offer you a deal to show you my goodwill."

What goodwill, you bloody bastard? Lotte thought but kept

her mouth shut, while she retreated to huddle against the wall with her eyes closed tight.

"If you become my willing mistress, *Schwester* Anna, I'll sign her death certificate. If not, I'll rape you anyway and then have you both executed. What's it going to be?"

Big, fat tears rolled down Lotte's cheeks as she shook her head, but Anna was already agreeing. "Fine. I'll be your mistress."

"Good girl." The doctor gave a satisfied chuckle, a sound that made her neck hair stand on end. "You and I will have plenty of fun. Now strip and look into my eyes."

Lotte pressed her hands over her ears and buried her head between her bony knees to block out any sound. Once started, her tears burst through an ever-widening breach in the dike of her resistance, bawling for every injustice she'd witnessed during the last four months. She wasn't sure how long she sat like this when Anna's voice caught her attention.

"The death certificate?"

"Since you were so compliant, it'll be my pleasure." The sound of a scratching plume emboldened Lotte to open her eyes again. The doctor was bent over the desk, writing something. "Here it is." He waved the paper in the air.

How fitting. The women were right. Cry today, you die tomorrow. Except, I'm already dead.

Anna didn't flinch when the doctor sauntered towards her. She held her head high and her shoulders straight, staring at him with hate-filled eyes. Lotte was amazed at the mental strength her sister possessed. *I was once like that. Before arriving in this hellish place.*

"I'll see you again real soon," Doctor Tretter said to Anna and gave her one last slap on her behind before he finally left.

"Anna, are you hurt?" Lotte scrambled to her feet, weeping for the sacrifice her sister had made.

"I will be fine," Anna answered and smoothed her hands down her nurse's uniform. She didn't cry, but Lotte knew her well enough to find the truth in her eyes. They hugged each other tight, both drawing comfort from each other. After several long moments, Anna pulled back and said, "It's time."

"Time for what?"

"To leave this place."

The silence was only filled by the mad beating of Lotte's heart as Anna led her baby sister to the wagon used to haul the corpses away. "What's going to happen?"

Anna placed her hands on her little sister's shoulders. "I'm afraid you have to get undressed first. Lie here very still and quiet. I'll cover you with a blanket to make things a little more bearable, but you have to pretend to be dead until the church bells chime midnight. Then you climb from the pit and escape via the far side. Ursula will be waiting for you."

Lotte looked at the wagon while she took off the detested blue-and-white striped dress. Then she glanced at her feet.

"The plimsolls you gave me for my birthday have served me well."

Anna looked up, a single tear sliding from an eye. "I wish you could keep them, but you know the drill. Ursula will have a dress and shoes for you on the other side."

Again, Lotte's eyes filled with tears, and she embraced her sister one last time before climbing onto the wagon. "Thank you so much, Anna. I couldn't have wished for two better sisters."

CHAPTER 26

Lotte lost track of time as the wagon rattled and bumped over the ground. She clenched her teeth, digging her nails into her palms to keep from struggling as she was dumped into the pit.

She heard the undertakers say a quick prayer over the dead bodies of their fellow prisoners, and the sound of the wagon being wheeled back inside the camp. Lotte lay there, a dead body draped across her legs, another splayed on her back. Somehow, she'd managed to turn as the wagon was dumped and had landed on her stomach, protecting her face and airway. The air was fetid, the smell causing her to gag, but her survival depended upon pretending to be dead.

She feared she would go mad as the hours crawled by, but she remained perfectly still until she could safely crawl out of the immense grave. After eleven o'clock, when all the prisoners had returned from their forced labor, the guards no longer patrolled the outside of the camp. She knew that was why Anna had arranged for her to flee the burial pit at midnight. Like a ghost, rising from the dead at the witching hour.

Lotte gave a dry laugh and counted the chimes of the church bell. One short one for every quarter of the hour. One longer one for every hour. One, two, three…nine, ten. Two more hours and she would make her move.

She lay among the dead, feeling as if she belonged, so weak and sick was she. But the hope of seeing Ursula and Mutter again instilled an inner strength she didn't know she still possessed. Lotte closed her eyes, allowing the vision of her mother and sisters to fill her mind. This would keep her awake because if she fell asleep, she'd miss the stroke of midnight – and her second chance at life.

Eleven.

Twelve.

It was time.

Lotte gathered her last ounce of strength and crawled, pushed, pulled, and climbed. Once she was on top of the pile of corpses, she faced a high earthen wall. She traveled in time back to Aunt Lydia's farm and how she'd raced her cousins Jörg and Helmut up the trees.

I can do this. I can. I must.

She sent up a prayer of forgiveness for stepping on the dead bodies nearest the wall and then used their corpses to give herself a boost up, digging her toes into the soft earth, kicking and clawing her way out of the pit.

Her nails were bleeding by the time she made it out, and she collapsed on the snow-covered ground, but only for a second.

Anna had told her, "You have fifteen minutes, twenty at

most. Ursula will arrive at a quarter past midnight, but she can't wait for long."

Lotte half walked, half crawled toward the metal fence surrounding the mass grave. Since nobody expected the dead to escape, it wasn't topped with barbed wire like the prison wall. It was almost too easy to traverse the fence, falling to the other side.

Her breath coming in spurts, she sensed her strength beginning to fail her. Without proper muscles to do the heavy work, every exercise became an almost insurmountable task. *At least I don't weigh much anymore.* When her pulse finally slowed down enough to make another move, she heard the damned church bell chime one time. A quarter past midnight.

"Hide in the copse of trees just ahead," Anna had explained.

It wasn't far, maybe a few hundred yards, but putting one foot in front of the other was one of the most challenging things she'd ever done. Every three or four steps, she had to catch her breath, but she never stopped, never faltered.

I must reach the copse. I will not give up. I will...

Lotte reached the trees and fell to the ground when a woman on a bicycle stopped in front of her.

"Here, take this and get on." Ursula handed her a woolen cape and pointed at the luggage rack on the back.

Lotte slipped the warm cape over her naked body and collapsed on the luggage rack, holding tight onto Ursula's hips as her sister quickly pedaled away. The ride passed in a blur, complete exhaustion taking over. Finally, Ursula stopped on the outskirts of town, and Lotte felt herself being carried to a small house where an older woman answered the door.

She was taken into the basement, laid on a small cot with a mattress, bed sheets, and a pillow – *what a wonderful soft pillow* – and covered with a warm blanket. Ursula returned and held a cup of chicken broth to her lips, making her swallow the hot liquid in tiny sips. Warmth seeped into her bones, and Lotte closed her eyes, letting sleep claim her battered body. The last sound she heard was the crackle of the fire in the stove.

I'm in a safe place.

~

The next morning, Lotte woke with a start, glaring at the unfamiliar room. She scratched her itching scalp.

Ursula peeked through the doorway. "Hey, sleepyhead. You're awake."

"Where are we?" Lotte pushed herself to a sitting position.

"At a friend's house. Are you hungry?"

Lotte nodded and then burst into tears. "I am. I want… can I wash up someplace? It's been so long."

"Of course, you can. Come on, I'll help you." Ursula helped her off the cot and led her to the bathroom, equipped with a tall tub and a sink with running water. Ursula filled the tub, laid a bar of soap on the edge, and then helped Lotte take her nightgown off.

Lotte glanced at the soft, white material. She didn't remember having put it on. All she remembered was the woolen cape Ursula had handed her before she mounted the bicycle. It didn't matter. Her modesty had long since fled, and she allowed Ursula to help her sink into the hot water.

"You have no idea how good this feels," Lotte murmured as she leaned back against the tub and then closed her eyes as the hot water began to work wonders on her sore body.

"No, I probably don't. And I don't want to trade places with you for one second." Ursula chuckled, but the sound was full of sympathy. "Lean up, and I'll wash your hair for you. Remember I used to do this when you were in kindergarten?"

"It's all falling out." Lotte glanced at a tuft of short hair swimming on the surface.

"Don't worry. It will grow back. You just need to eat the right food and get enough rest. It will come back, more beautiful than before."

"It's turning gray, too," Lotte murmured, wondering how many other seventeen-year olds had gray hair.

Again, Ursula chuckled. "No, Lotte. Not turning gray, just dirty and full of ash from the crematorium. It will wash out, you'll see."

Ursula gently washed her head, using a special soap designed to kill lice, and then gave her the privacy to wash her body unobserved for the first time in almost four months. After a few minutes, Ursula returned, bringing some of her own clothes with her. She helped Lotte from the tub and handed her a clean towel with which to dry herself. Lotte made quick work of that task and then stepped into the underwear Ursula handed her.

She'd not worn any since arriving at the camp, and recovering that little bit of privacy was overwhelming. Her tears threatened to flow again. Since when had she become such a crybaby? Lotte pulled herself together and allowed her sister to help her get dressed. Despite her being a good three inches taller than Ursula, her sister's dress bagged on her.

"Look at the scarecrow I am. I've lost so much weight," Lotte mumbled as she looked at her reflection in the mirror.

Ursula stood beside her and wrapped an arm around her shoulders. "You'll gain it back. You're alive and free, that's what matters."

Lotte's sigh was interrupted by a growl coming from her stomach. "You mentioned food?"

Ursula laughed. "Yes, but I don't want you to eat too much to start with. You'll get sick if you do."

The older woman had already set the table for Lotte. The hearty smell of chicken broth hung in the air and made Lotte's mouth water.

"Did I die last night and go to heaven?" Lotte licked her lips and reverently dunked the spoon into the broth with generous drops of grease swimming on top. "Hmmmmm… this is delicious."

She forced herself not to pick up the bowl and consume it in one swallow. By the time she emptied her bowl and carefully chewed the pieces of potato and chicken inside, her stomach was so full it almost hurt. Lotte eyed the slice of bread and butter and sniffed to take in the aroma of freshly baked bread. *Fresh bread. Real butter. Just like at Aunt Lydia's.*

Tears sprang to her eyes, and she touched the bread to feel the soft and flexible texture, held it to her nose to smell the distinctive aroma, and finally took a tiny bite, savoring the salty butter melting on her tongue. Then she chewed the soft fluffy bread several times until the yeasty, slightly bitter flavor turned sweet.

She leaned back and looked at her sister. "I'm full."

"You can finish the rest later. There's plenty where that came from."

Lotte reached for Ursula's hand. "Thanks for everything."

"That's what sisters are there for, right?" Ursula gazed at her with love in her eyes.

Lotte was filled with questions, and now that her belly was full, she had the strength to ask them. "How did you even find me?"

"Aunt Lydia called Mutter to let us know you had disappeared. It was quite a shock." Ursula pushed a strand of blonde hair behind her ear.

Lotte was the only sibling who'd inherited their grandmother's red mane of curls. Well, it had been curls. Now it looked more like grayish-red plucked plumage.

There was a certain nostalgia in Ursula's glance as she remembered the phone call from her aunt. Lotte sensed that there was something more, something she hadn't told, but for once she let it go. If Ursula wanted her to know, she'd tell her in due time.

"Aunt Lydia saw how you were pushed into the police car–"

"So it was her standing behind the window. Is she all right?" Lotte asked with bated breath.

"Yes." Ursula patted Lotte's arm. "Two weeks after you were arrested, she delivered the baby. It's a girl. Rosa."

Lotte smiled.

"Herr Keller apparently tried to take her farm away, but

since Uncle Peter and she are good friends with the leader of the farmer's association, he didn't succeed. But Aunt Lydia couldn't prevent him from arresting you that night. She had to think of her children."

"I know. And I'm so sorry for causing her so much trouble."

"The next day, she went down to the police station to plead with Herr Keller to set you free, but you weren't there anymore. He never told us what happened, and we feared the worst."

Uwe. At the memory of him, tears shot into Lotte's eyes.

"Several weeks later, we found out that you'd been sent to Ravensbrück." Ursula sighed. "Mutter didn't take it well. She had a breakdown."

"Good grief. How is she now?" Lotte couldn't imagine her mother being weak. Since she was a child, her mother had always been a force to reckon with, keeping four children – and a husband – under control with little more than a stern glance and a few well-chosen words.

Many times, Lotte had thought Mutter was way too strict, forbidding everything that was fun, warning her time and again not to speak imprudently and not to act rashly. *I should have followed her advice.*

"She doesn't know yet. Anna and I thought it best to tell her only after we rescued you, to avoid yet another disappointment. We have tried everything to get you transferred to a normal prison, but to no avail. With every failure, Mutter retreated more into herself."

Lotte felt the heavy burden of guilt for causing so much suffering to her mother.

"Then we got news about Vater and Richard. After not

talking to anyone for days, Mutter stopped leaving the house, except for going to the allotments."

"Are they...?" Lotte didn't dare say the word.

"Vater is a prisoner of war in Russia, and as far as we've been told, he is alive. But Richard is missing in action. The last time he was seen was somewhere near Minsk."

Lotte pressed her hands to her stomach, grief threatening to bring its contents up. "Minsk? Where is that?"

"I had to look it up in my atlas. It's in Belarus, about six hundred miles east of Berlin." Ursula smiled sadly, patting her sister's hand. "Mutter blames herself for your fate because she sent you away."

Lotte's eyes widened. Her mother believed that?

CHAPTER 27

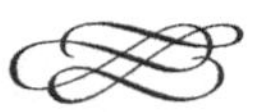

"I'm so proud of you, Lotte."

Lotte couldn't believe her own ears. "Proud? There was nothing especially brave or prudent I've done." She had expected a lecture about her irresponsible behavior, but praise? Coming from Ursula, who'd never broken a rule in her life?

"Don't say that. We found out about the Jews in hiding and the fake papers." Ursula's blue eyes rested on her with the kind of pride only an older sister could show.

"I don't regret having helped them. But I do wish I had planned things better." Lotte took a sip from the glass of cold, whole milk in front of her and then licked around her mouth like a cat so as not to waste a single drop.

"Yes, you should have. But that doesn't matter now. What matters is that you did the right thing, and you're here to tell the tale." Ursula ruffled her cropped hair.

"Who are you and what did you do to my sister, impostor?" Lotte teased. The Ursula she knew would never condone an illegal action, morally justified or not. Hiding Jews and faking papers definitely fell into that category.

"A lot has happened in the past few months, and I have changed." Ursula laughed.

"I am watching in awe. How could you even be so bold as to try and rescue me? Isn't that against the law, helping a prisoner escape?" Lotte wanted to run a hand through her hair but stopped midway. She'd given up that habit months ago to keep her hands free of lice and filth.

"Well, let's say I had an epiphany and decided that some laws should be broken."

Lotte stared at her sister, disbelief in her eyes.

"Yes, I joined an underground network hiding Jews and helping them escape to safe zones."

"You do what?" Lotte shook her head. Had the entire world turned upside down while she vegetated in the camp? "Ursula, you have to be careful."

Her sister smirked. "Look who's talking. Don't worry, we're very cautious. Always."

"Does Mutter know?"

Ursula's smile turned sly. "Let's just say she's a tacit accomplice, by pretending not to notice that we take provisions from the pantry and use the shed in our allotment garden to hide people for a few days at a time."

"Gee whiz! I'm in hell several months, and when I return to earth, it's not a globe anymore? You work as a subversive and Mother looks the other way. What else don't I know?"

"A lot. So many things have happened in the past four months." Ursula sighed.

"Four months...it feels more like four lifetimes." Lotte's voice trailed off, her eyes looking at the wall, not sure whether her sister expected her to give an account of the conditions in the camp. "It was so awful. Dehumanizing. Reduced to a number, an object to exploit and torture. I can't...I can't bear to talk about it now."

"You don't have to, sweetie, not now. You need to forget and let your body heal. We have enough other sources to tell us what's happening in the camp. Anna, for example."

"Anna!" Lotte screamed and jumped up, sending her chair crashing to the ground. How could she have forgotten about Anna?

"What about Anna?" Ursula's hand flew to her throat.

Lotte wrung her hands and started to weep as she remembered the look in Anna's eyes after the doctor had...

She sniffed and looked at Ursula. "Anna sacrificed...the doctor, he found out we were sisters, and he...he raped her!"

"You were there?" Ursula asked, horrified.

Lotte nodded and lowered her voice to a whisper. "He forced her to become his mistress in exchange for his silence."

Ursula thinned her lips and sat up a little straighter. "She knew about the risks involved."

"We have to help her," Lotte cried, guilt over her sister's sacrifice heavy on her mind.

"No. Anna will have to deal with it on her own. We can't risk any rash actions that might endanger not only you and her but everyone involved in your rescue." Ursula picked up the chair and placed it beside the table again.

"There were more people involved?"

"Yes. Many more. That's why we can't do anything for Anna right now."

Lotte thought it was cruel and callous to let Anna fend

for herself, but Ursula was probably right. She inhaled deeply several times. "What happens now?"

"I have something for you." Ursula gave her a soft smile. "Come with me."

Lotte followed her back into the basement and plopped on the bed while Ursula disappeared to fetch something. She was tired but sated. For the first time in months, the gnawing in her insides had disappeared.

She raised a hand and carefully touched her straw-like hair. It felt surprisingly soft. She ran the hand along her entire head and then looked at her fingertips. Clean. Only then did she notice the absence of another constant companion during the last months – the itching and biting. She really had been born again.

Ursula returned and handed Lotte an *Ausweis*. She turned it over and gasped at the healthy young woman with curly red hair looking at her. *That's me!*

It was a brand-new identification card in the name of Alexandra Wagner, born on February 28, 1926. She caressed the paper with her thumb. Unlike so many others who had perished, she'd been given a second chance at life.

"Where did you get that photograph?" Lotte asked her sister.

Ursula's face darkened. "At my wedding almost one year ago."

"How can I ever thank you for everything you did for me?" Lotte was touched to her very soul.

"Thank me by recovering fast and staying the compassionate, outspoken, and justice-loving young woman you are." Ursula gave her a bear hug, and Lotte noticed with some jealousy her sister's full bosom as well as her rounded hips and belly. Her own breasts had been reduced to hanging flaps of skin.

"What about Andreas?" Lotte asked. She couldn't see her sister's face in their embrace, but she felt the slumping of her shoulders.

"He's gone."

"Gone? He hasn't returned from the front since your wedding?" Lotte's mind didn't work as swiftly as it had done before her incarceration.

"He's dead. Killed in action."

"I'm so sorry." Lotte held her sister tighter.

"He died last May. I should have told you earlier, but I couldn't bring myself to say the words. I guess I somehow believed he would come back if I didn't acknowledge his death." Ursula released her and stood from the bed. "You should rest. When you're hungry, come upstairs. The blackout curtains will always be closed so nobody will see you."

CHAPTER 28

Lotte remained in the custody of the landlady while Ursula returned to Berlin the next day. For two solid weeks, she didn't do much more than sleep and eat. Looking like a skeleton, she wasn't allowed outside – the danger of being spotted as a camp prisoner was too great.

After putting on ten pounds and a fashionable haircut – courtesy of the landlady – Ursula's clothes still bagged on her, but Lotte had begun to look like a human being again.

It was time to leave the town of Ravensbrück and recover in a safe place far away, where nobody would suspect her to be an escapee or recognize her as the "deceased" Lotte Klausen.

Alexandra Wagner. Her new name was still unfamiliar, but at least her sisters had been considerate enough to use her middle name. What she was excited about was her new birthday. In less than a month, she would be of age. A smile appeared on her lips. Like every adolescent, she'd yearned for that day, and now it would arrive seven months early.

Ursula returned, and together they would travel to Berlin. Home. But Lotte knew she couldn't stay there. Her sister had promised a safe place where she could hide and recover for as long as necessary.

While Lotte burned with hatred for the Nazis more than ever and longed to do her bit in fighting them, she also accepted the fact that in her current condition she wouldn't be of much use to their cause. For now, she was excited at the prospect of seeing Mutter before departing to another godforsaken town.

"What's up, Lotte? Ready to leave this town?" Ursula greeted her.

"More than you can imagine." Lotte grinned at her sister. Every day she had gained weight and strength, and now felt full of energy. Wrapped in a thick winter coat and long woolen gloves, a smart hat on her head, she followed Ursula to the railway station.

Memories of her arrival here assailed her, and her heart started racing. Her sister must have sensed her inner tumult, because she linked arms with her and whispered, "It's fine. Everything's fine."

Once onboard the train to Berlin Gesundbrunnen, Lotte managed to breathe again. During the three-hour journey, she marveled at the difference between this one and the one in the cattle train when she'd arrived months ago. A shudder ran down her spine, that intensified in the next moment when a conductor entered to punch their tickets, followed by SS to check on their papers.

She blinked and forced her hand to remain still as she handed over her new identification. The SS man looked at the two sisters – who weren't sisters anymore, but close friends – up and down and then left.

Lotte slumped back in her seat. Her papers had passed the acid test.

As they arrived at Berlin Gesundbrunnen, she spied her mother waiting on the platform. *She looks old and afflicted.*

"Charlotte! Oh, my precious girl. Look at you! You've lost so much weight. And your beautiful hair."

"Mutter, she's Alexandra," Ursula whispered and cast a warning glare. "She's alive. All the rest will fix itself with time."

"I know. I just wasn't expecting this. Well, no matter. You're here now. I'm so happy to see you." Mutter grabbed Lotte into a tight hug.

Lotte wrapped her arms around Mutter. Something about being in her mother's arms again peeled so many layers of heartache away. Her mother pulled back from her and stood on her tiptoes to smooth a hand over Lotte's cheek, kissing her cheeks and then hugging her once again. It was a rather unusual display of physical affection.

"Mutter. Alexandra. We should resume this reunion somewhere more private," Ursula suggested, seeing that they were beginning to draw attention to themselves. Even though Lotte's fake papers had withstood the scrutiny of an SS man, it wouldn't do to draw unnecessary attention from the Gestapo or other government officials walking around the train station.

"Yes, we should go someplace where we can talk." Lotte broke away from her mother. She needed a chance to convince Mutter that what happened next was for the best of everyone involved.

At first, she'd fought against Ursula's suggestion with tooth and nail, but after thinking over the options, she realized there weren't that many. She couldn't live with either Mutter or Aunt Lydia, or any relative for that matter, and risk being recognized as Charlotte Klausen.

The Mother Reverend of the convent in Kaufbeuren had kindly agreed to accept Lotte/Alexandra into her orphanage for as long as she wanted to stay. Of course, the nuns would never openly say so, but their convent played an important role in the underground network Ursula worked for.

While Ursula wished for Lotte to stay in the safety of the convent until the war was over, Lotte herself had different plans. But her next attempt to oppose the regime would be built on a solid foundation.

They walked to a small bakery across the street, and Lotte gasped several times at the utter destruction around her. Rubble wherever she looked, gray faces of despairing women and men struggling to clear the streets of debris.

At the bakery, they ordered pancakes and *Ersatzkaffee*.

"That pseudo-coffee is barely drinkable," Ursula complained.

Lotte cocked her head. "You should have tasted the putrid dishwater they gave us for coffee."

"Sorry," Ursula said as both she and Mutter gave a sheepish look. "I guess then *Ersatzkaffee* is a delicacy."

After about half an hour, Ursula pointed at her watch and gave Lotte an encouraging nod. Lotte inwardly groaned. Now came the hardest part.

"Mutter, I don't have much time," Lotte began, the words catching in her throat.

"What? You're not staying?" Mutter's eyes darted between her two daughters. "What haven't you told me?"

"It's not safe. We've talked about this, Mutter." Ursula came to Lotte's aid.

"Yes. And I understand that with nosy Frau Weber living next to us, Charl..." She shook her head at her slip. "Alexandra can't come home. But I thought she would at least stay in Berlin, where I can watch over her. The last time I sent her away didn't work out so well." Mutter seemed to shrink with every word she spoke.

"Mutter." Lotte sidled up to her mother and took her hands into her own. "What happened was entirely my own fault. There's nothing you could have done to prevent it."

Mutter gave a small smile, but her eyes filled with sorrow.

Lotte's heart gave a hard squeeze. "My train leaves in twenty minutes."

"Where are you going?" Mutter murmured.

"Someplace safe," Ursula said. "She'll stay there until things change. But she'll be safe. I promise."

Lotte squeezed her mother's hand. "This is for the best. I can be of so much help there while I would just be a liability here. If anyone were to ever discover what Ursula and Anna did...we would all be in hot water."

"Will you at least write?"

"If I can." Lotte hadn't discussed communicating with her mother or the ramifications of doing so with Ursula. Because of her sisters, she'd been given a second chance at life, and the foolhardiness of the past was dead and buried. From now on she would always act with purpose and a well thought out plan. The consequences of doing things rashly were too horrific to bear a second time.

"Godspeed you," Mutter said and hugged her one last time. "Be well."

"I will." *More than you can imagine.*

A whistle sounded, and Ursula said, "That's your train. You need to get on board."

"I love you, Mutter. Take care and don't worry about me. I'm going to be fine." Lotte picked up the small bag Ursula had given her. It contained a few changes of clothing, none of which fit her, but Ursula had assured her the nuns would have everything she needed to alter them when she arrived at the convent.

The next day, she arrived at the train station in Kaufbeuren. A slight worry entered her mind as she tried to remember how to get to the convent. But much to her delight, two nuns were waiting for her on the platform. Lotte smiled hesitantly and then followed them as they walked the few blocks to their destination.

"Thank you for meeting me," she said as they walked down a nearly deserted street.

"No thanks are necessary," one of the nuns replied. Several minutes later, they arrived at the convent where two young boys rushed down the stairwell to meet her.

"Hello!" they called out.

"How are you?" Rachel's brothers had grown quite a bit during the past months and seemed to cope considerably well with the loss of their parents and sisters.

"We are good. You've been sick?" Israel asked.

Lotte started to shake her head, then nodded instead.

There was no reason for these young children to know the atrocities that were taking place in Germany. Let them keep whatever innocence they still possessed. "I am getting better. I've come to stay with you for a while."

"Good. That is good," Israel said, pulling his brother by the arm, "The girls' rooms are this way."

"Thank you." Lotte followed the nun to the girls' quarters with a smile on her face. The two boys wandered off to play in the gardens.

Her new home was a rather large room on the upper floor of a side building of the convent. It was equipped with twenty-four bunk beds and several cribs. Lotte wouldn't have much privacy here either, but she had an entire bed with a mattress, bed sheets, pillow, and a blanket all to herself.

Attached to the dormitory was a bathroom with six showers and six lavatories. And to the other side were the toilets. Every girl was assigned a small drawer to store her belongings.

The nun broke into Lotte's appreciation of the room. "Those two have adapted quite well. They seem to have come to terms with their situation. God be blessed."

"They look happy."

"They are during the day, but at night, we often hear them cry." The nun turned to leave. "Take your time getting settled, you'll be introduced to everyone during lunch."

Lotte decided there was no time like the present to take care of her hardest task. "Sister, could you please tell me where I might find Sister Margarete?"

A brow lifted. "You know her?"

"We met several months ago, and I would like to greet her."

The nun smiled and pointed out the window. "She is in the prayer garden at this time every day. If you go back down the stairs and go to your left, you'll find a door leading you to the garden."

"Thank you, Sister."

"You are most welcome."

Lotte inhaled deeply a few more times and stowed her few belongings in the drawer she'd been assigned before setting off down the stairwell, searching for the entrance to the prayer garden.

Sister Margarete was sitting in silence before a large fountain, dry now because it was still winter, but nonetheless beautiful. Lotte turned up her collar as a chilly gust swept through, grateful for the protection her winter coat offered.

"Sister Margarete?" she asked softly.

The nun raised her head, and her eyes opened wide as she recognized her. "Charlotte, right? Uwe's friend. The one who recommended Peter and Klaus to us."

Peter and Klaus? Lotte frowned. "Actually, my name is Alexandra." *Oh yes, Israel and Aron have new names, too. I completely forgot.*

"Please sit." Sister Margarete invited her without any further comment, but her bright blue eyes made it clear she knew. Knew that Peter and Klaus weren't the real names of the two boys. Knew the reason why their sisters hadn't made it to the convent. Knew why Charlotte was Alexandra.

Lotte cleared her throat. "I wanted to come and tell you in person how sorry I am about Uwe."

"He is with God now." Sister Margarete's voice softened at the memory of her nephew.

"Yes, but...but it was my fault. They killed him because he was helping me." Lotte's eyes filled with tears. She hadn't had the opportunity to grieve. In the camp, tears meant weakness and weakness meant death, so she'd pushed thoughts of Uwe away whenever they entered her mind. But here, so near to where they'd experienced sweet love, she couldn't hold her tears back.

"Alexandra, know this...it wasn't your fault." Sister Margarete looked at her with compassion in her eyes. "We do not always understand God's plans, but everything happens for a reason. Uwe made his own decisions, and I have faith that he did what he thought was right. He wouldn't want you to feel guilty for actions he took of his own free will. He would want you to forgive yourself. There is nothing to be gained from carrying around guilt over something you cannot change or rectify. Be at peace and know that he is also at peace."

A flood of tears rushed down Lotte's face. "I'm sorry, Sister. It seems all I do these days is cry."

The nun wrapped an arm around her shoulders and took her hands with her free one. "For what you've suffered, you have every right to cry. Weep as often as you like, and then let the emotions that created the tears help you to right what wrongs you can. We can't let this war destroy all that is godly, decent, and human within us. We have to be stronger than the evil sent to tempt us."

Lotte appreciated the nun's words, and she closed her eyes, offering up a prayer for the souls of the dead and for those who were still suffering.

The Nazis had tried to annihilate her, but she had survived.

~

Thank you so much for taking the time to read WAR GIRL LOTTE.

If you enjoyed the book would you do me a huge favor and leave me a review? I'd really, really appreciate it:

The next book in the series is WAR GIRL ANNA. Anna is left in an awful situation as the mistress of a man she despises. Will she be able to find a way to save herself without endangering her sister and the entire resistance network?

Order here: War Girl Lotte

If this is the first of my books you've read, you might want to continue with War Girl Ursula, the first in series. All War Girl books can be read as standalone, although some readers prefer to read in order.

Signup to my newsletter to be the first one to hear about new releases. As a subscriber you'll receive my free short story DOWNED OVER GERMANY, the prequel to the War Girl Series.

Tom Westlake, a British RAF pilot survives when his plane is shot down. But being stranded behind enemy lines is only the beginning of his nightmare.

http://kummerow.info/newsletter-2

AUTHOR'S NOTES

Dear Reader,

Thanks so much for reading WAR GIRL LOTTE.

If you've read War Girl Ursula, you probably knew that Lotte was a disaster waiting to happen. Her love of justice and outspokenness would sooner or later get her into trouble.

Ravensbrück was the only concentration camp exclusively for women (although in 1941 a small section for men was added), and at the same time it is the most forgotten camp in history, since it was "only" a concentration camp, meant to punish the inmates, not a death camp like Auschwitz or Treblinka. It was also one of the few camps, where the majority of the inmates wasn't Jewish, for the simple reason that Jews were sent to Auschwitz to be gassed.

"Ravensbrück was an abomination that the world has resolved to forget." (Francois Mauriac).

War Girl Lotte wants to help remember the unfortunate women who were forced to live and die there.

Unfortunately the heinous medical experiments on the *Króliki*, or rabbits, 86 mostly Polish women, did really happen. Dr. Karl Gebhardt, who was not only Chief surgeon in the SS, but also Heinrich Himmler's personal physician, oversaw these horrific experiments that happened in Ravensbrück from July 1942 to August 1943.

I did bend the timeline slightly to extend the medical experiments to the end of 1943 when Lotte's story takes place.

You can read more here: http://ahrp.org/ravensbruck-young-girls-subjected-to-grotesque-medical-atrocities/

Another true event that I used for my storyline was the typhus vaccine. Eugeniusz Sławomir Łazowski, a Polish physician, managed to save 8,000 Jews from being deported to one of the concentration camps. His trick was to inject them with dead typhus cells (a vaccine), that would make them immune to the sickness, but when a blood sample was taken, they would test positive for the dreaded disease.

The Nazis were deathly afraid of an epidemic of typhus fever (transmitted by lice), because it was difficult to contain and had killed hundreds of thousands of soldiers and civilians during WW1. Rather than risk being contaminated while handling the transport to extermination camps, they preferred to quarantine the infected and let the disease do their ghastly work.

https://www.warhistoryonline.com/world-war-ii/polish-doctor-created-fake-typhus-epidemic-saved-8000-jews-wwii-xb.html

ALSO BY MARION KUMMEROW

Love and Resistance in WW2 Germany

Unrelenting

Unyielding

Unwavering

Turning Point (Spin-off)

War Girl Series

Downed over Germany (Prequel)

War Girl Ursula (Book 1)

War Girl Lotte (Book 2)

War Girl Anna (Book 3)

Reluctant Informer (Book 4)

Trouble Brewing (Book 5)

Fatal Encounter (Book 6)

Uncommon Sacrifice (Book 7)

Bitter Tears (Book 8)

Secrets Revealed (Book 9)

Together at Last (Book 10)

Endless Ordeal (Book 11)

Berlin Fractured

From the Ashes (Book 1)

On the Brink (Book 2)

Historical Romance

Second Chance at First Love

Find all my books here:

http://www.kummerow.info

CONTACT ME

I truly appreciate you taking the time to read (and enjoy) my books. And I'd be thrilled to hear from you!
If you'd like to get in touch with me you can do so via

Twitter:
http://twitter.com/MarionKummerow

Facebook:
http://www.facebook.com/AutorinKummerow

Website
http://www.kummerow.info

Made in the USA
Coppell, TX
28 January 2021